Brotherhood of Blood

One & Only

BIANCA D'ARC

This book is a work of fiction. The names, characters, places, and incidents are products of the writer's imagination or have been used fictitiously and are not to be construed as real. Any resemblance to persons, living or dead, actual events, locale or organizations is entirely coincidental.

No part of this book may be used or reproduced in any manner whatsoever without written permission, except in the case of brief quotations embodied in critical articles and reviews.

DEDICATION &
AUTHOR'S NOTE

First, a little note about this new edition of the very first paranormal romance story I ever had accepted for publication. The original version of this story was written for a writing competition, and was strictly limited to a mere 5,000 words according to the rules of the contest. It did not win, but it gained the attention of a small press publisher who offered a contract for publication out of the blue. I was thrilled!

One & Only first saw the light of day as that small, 5,000 word contest *Honorable Mention* and started me down the path of writing vampires, werecreatures of all kinds, and things that go bump in the night. When that small publisher went out of business, I was able to move this story, and its sequels, over to Samhain Publishing. By doing so, I was finally able to expand the stories to something quite a bit longer and more developed, and they were all republished, starting in 2008.

Now, for the first time, I am able to put them into print individually. Samhain was able to publish a print anthology that had all of the first three novellas in it back in 2009, but this publication marks the first time any of them have been available in a separate print edition.

The follow-up stories, **Rare Vintage** and **Phantom Desires**, will be republished in 2016 as they come due for a revamp (pardon the pun) and rerelease. Meanwhile, I hope you will enjoy the updated version of **One & Only** that follows.

And the original dedication still stands…

To my family. For believing in my dream, even when I didn't.

CHAPTER ONE

What was that noise? It was subtle, yet it grated on the ancient one's sensitive hearing. A metallic *twang-slap-grind* that set his teeth on edge and made him wonder just how mechanically sound this old shuttle bus really was.

Once again, he marveled at how a being as powerful as he still needed to conform to the expectations of mortals—especially in the brave new world of technology. It was becoming harder and harder to reinvent himself now that his image was captured routinely in a myriad of different official ways. The next time he had to "die" and come back, he'd have to alter his appearance drastically. Mortal memories might be short, but photographs, it seemed, lived forever.

Of course, that was supposing he'd bother to come back this time.

Atticus Maxwell had been alive longer than he believed any being rightly should. The centuries had become endless. The business of living was tedious, with no one to share it with. Atticus had always been a loner, but had always held the secret hope that someday he would find at least one person in all the world—and all the centuries—to share his life.

It was the dearest goal of many of his kind. After a few centuries, most bloodletters settled down and began the search for the one person who could complete them. It was a serious business, and a quest he didn't take lightly, but after so many years, he'd pretty much given up hope.

Atticus had searched longer than most, but he was still alone.

Lissa hadn't wanted to board the shuttle bus, but there was no other feasible way to get to the rustic mountain retreat where a business conference she had to attend was being held. The place was on a rocky hillside that bordered wine country. The views were said to be magnificent and the five-star cuisine was not to be missed. Or so the travel agent had promised.

Lissa was at a crossroads in her career, having just lost her job as an account manager due to company downsizing. This conference was supposed to help her network for new contacts in her field and also had the advantage of hosting a small job fair of sorts. She had two interviews lined up for tomorrow, in fact, but she couldn't seem to shake the feeling of foreboding that had enveloped her when she boarded the hotel's private shuttle bus.

It happened that way sometimes. Lissa had a very small psychic gift that had helped her avoid trouble in the past, but tonight she was getting mixed signals from her sixth sense. She didn't want to board the bus, but she didn't know if that apprehensive knot in the bottom of her stomach was due to the shuttle bus itself, the passengers on it with her, or the conference that awaited her.

Then he'd appeared.

A man. Out of the night. He'd stolen her breath, and all her senses—both mystical and mundane—had gone on alert. He was dangerous. She could tell that, just by the aura of power that surrounded him. But he was also the most handsome and enticing being she had ever encountered.

Her sixth sense pulled her toward him. It made her yearn for him in a way she had never yearned before. Something about him was both arresting and fearsome at the same time, yet he drew her as a moth to a flame, and she was powerless to resist his allure.

So she boarded the bus. She allowed herself to be drawn in. She'd even encroached on his personal space to the point where he stumbled over her foot, crushing her toes for a short moment while her cheeks flamed in embarrassment.

"I'm so sorry," he said as he stumbled. Alarmed blue eyes met her gaze for a brief moment as shock passed over his features. "Please excuse me."

His voice rolled over her, rich and deep. It rumbled through her very being, awakening every synapse in that brief moment that was over all too soon. She smiled at him and mumbled her acknowledgment, but he'd already turned to claim his seat farther back in the crowded shuttle bus.

And that was the extent of their contact.

So little to build such a lasting impression. Lissa knew she would never forget the man as long as she lived, though she would probably never even know his name.

Atticus pondered the small woman he had unwittingly touched. She was a drab little thing in her buttoned up navy blue suit, but there was something very appealing about her. He had sought the mountain retreat that overlooked his own land in the valley far below for a bit of peace, but his thoughts were in more turmoil now than they had been in many decades.

Who was that woman? And why did she claim so much of his attention?

He really should be concentrating more on the strange sounds coming from the van's undercarriage, but he couldn't bring himself to look away from her. He could just see the top of her head over the top of the seat a few rows in front of him. She had lustrous brown hair he wanted to feel under his fingers.

Lightning flashed close by, distracting him, and the bus swerved on the slick mountain road. The driver pumped the brakes and the grinding sound elevated to a screeching metallic twang ending with a sickening snap. Quick as that lightning flash, the bus slid sideways on the wet pavement, overturned, then tumbled over the edge of the ribbon of road, into the void.

The shuttle bus rolled violently down the steep ravine. Atticus was thrown from side-to-side, top-to-bottom in a violent thrashing of metal against soft tissue that had no chance at all against such devastation.

The shuttle bus came to rest, after long moments of sickening freefall, at the bottom of a cliff, deep in wet foliage. The only sound was the creaking of metal as it rocked to a stop and the steady drip of soft rain on the leaves of the forest.

He was going to die.

Finally, after over a thousand years of walking the earth, his life was going to end. Atticus almost welcomed it.

But the girl would die, too, and that bothered him. He thought it odd. By now he probably shouldn't have a conscience left, but the thought of her death—when he could, in all likelihood, save her—plagued him.

His worries seemed very far away while lying in a pool of his own blood, with some kind of support beam making a hole in his chest. Atticus felt his immortal life slipping away, but the faint, struggling gasps for breath issuing from the small woman called him back. She was alive. For the moment.

Everyone else on the shuttle bus was dead. Atticus knew they were gone when their heartbeats ceased echoing in his ears. He no longer sensed the motion of their blood swishing through their veins.

They were all gone. All except for the quiet girl who had smiled so kindly at him after he'd accidentally stepped on her foot while boarding.

Atticus never touched mortals, except to feed. Such acute hearing and senses sometimes made it painful to get within touching distance of them, unless they were under his thrall. Yet, somehow, this quiet, shy woman had invaded his personal space earlier that night. She had crept up on him without his knowledge. Or perhaps it was Atticus who had invaded her space. He couldn't be sure. But whichever way it happened, it had shocked him.

He hadn't been so surprised in years. Centuries even.

Yet this nondescript woman, with the soft-looking, mousy brown hair and hazel eyes, somehow managed to invade not only his space, but his thoughts as well.

Incredible.

And now she would die, alone in the night, on the side of a deserted mountain road, along with the rest of them.

Unless he fought against the darkness. And won.

Regardless of what he was, with such injuries as he'd already sustained, it would not be an easy battle.

CHAPTER TWO

When Lissa Adams woke, darkness engulfed her. Straining to see in the absence of light, her breath accelerated as she panicked. She was laying down. She could feel an uneven surface against her back.

Her apprehension grew when she realized another person lay beside her. A soft dripping sound echoed through what she supposed was some kind of underground chamber or cave. That's what it sounded like—and smelled like. She felt rough rock and scattered grains of sandy dirt beneath her palms.

She knew the mountains were dotted with such places, but she couldn't remember how she'd gotten here. Or why she was so groggy.

She tried to sit up, but the effort it required nearly blacked her out again. The being beside her stirred at her movement, and she felt more than saw the person rise to lean over her.

"Where are we?"

"I moved us to shelter."

Rich and warm, his voice bathed her senses in a dark and dangerous way.

Sexy, she thought. She'd heard that voice before.

The memory of it was accompanied by flashing blue eyes and chiseled features. A man's face flickered through her mind. She'd been fascinated by him and instantly captivated. She remembered thinking he was quite possibly the most striking man she'd ever seen.

"You stepped on my foot." Her voice was weak to her own ears.

He chuckled at her innocent observation, setting her insides aflame.

"Indeed. But that was more than twenty-four hours ago."

He stroked a gentle finger down her cheek and she shivered, not in fear, but in surprising arousal. If just the brush of his finger on her face could elicit this response, she wondered what he could do if he really tried.

That thought stopped her cold. Men like

this one didn't usually go for women like her. Better to focus on the peculiar situation she found herself in than daydream about her rescuer.

"What happened? I remember the bus swerving…"

"Ah, yes. Just before we rolled down the side of the mountain. You hit your head very hard, I'm afraid. That's probably why you're still a bit fuzzy."

"Where's everyone else?"

He paused only slightly. "Dead."

Her breath caught in shock as her mind raced. "How did we…?"

"Relax, sweetheart." He moved closer. "I pulled you from the wreckage and found shelter, but I was badly damaged in the accident as well. I'm sorry for it, but I need your essence to speed my healing."

"My what?" Hot breath bathed her ear as he settled closer to her side. His strong arms enveloped her shoulders as his mouth stroked over the line of her jaw and lower.

"Don't be afraid. I won't hurt you, but I need your blood, and I'm too weak to cloud your mind. You'll have to trust me." His words whispered against her shivering skin. He dragged sharp teeth back and forth over

11

her jugular as if savoring the moment before the feast.

She barely had time to take in his words before he struck. A piercing pain registered only for a flash, followed by the greatest bliss she had ever experienced. Intensely sexual, it engulfed her in a way she'd never known. He sucked at her neck, licking at the essence of her, swallowing like a thirsty man in the desert. Yet reverence and gentleness communicated through his tender handling of her bruised and battered body.

Oddly, she didn't object. She knew she should be afraid, but an intense arousal overwhelmed her. She didn't have the strength to voice even the faintest protest.

He drank for what seemed a long time, his hands moving over her body, molding her breasts and stroking her skin. Only then did she realize she was naked. She gasped as his long fingers stroked down between her legs, angling inward, invading her most intimate places as his mouth caressed the tender skin of her throat.

He knew his way around a woman's body. Those skilled fingers knew just where to stroke, just where to pinch to drive her excitement to the highest possible point. She teetered on the precipice as his fingers slid in the arousal he drew from her body. His mouth sucked at her neck, his breath feathering through her hair, his pleasing masculine scent teasing her senses. And the feel of him. He was hot and heavy against her, hard as only a man could be and muscular in a way she hadn't expected.

One hand cupped her breast, teasing her nipple as his fingers finally pierced the imaginary boundary, sliding inside her, where few men had ever been. But this man—though she'd known him only a few minutes, really—was like no other man she'd ever encountered. He fired her senses like no other, sending slick, hot arousal to her core. Even the thought that he was some sort of dark creature out of legend couldn't stop the most intense sexual experience of her life.

That one tantalizing finger pumped into her, stretching her. He added a second digit as she whimpered in need. She hadn't had sex in a long time. She was tight, but her body remembered pleasure, and this man— this vampire!—proved himself a master at manipulating her responses. He *owned* her pleasure.

Two long fingers stroked within, his

thumb teased higher, rubbing in perfect counterpoint. She came with a wrenching jerk of hips that threatened to dislodge him, but his great strength kept her easily in his clutches. He continued the stimulation, extending her orgasm for long, intense moments while his upper body covered hers, his lips feeding hungrily from the small incisions he'd made in her neck. The pleasure washed over her in the most intense waves she'd ever known and right then she didn't care if he was a vampire, werewolf or Indian chief. All she knew was his mastery. And she already knew she wanted more.

Gods! She was sweet. The sweetest woman he'd had in all his many centuries.

And he'd had many.

Temptation lured him to drain her dry and take all of her precious essence, but he hadn't gone through the trouble of saving her—and himself—for nothing. He'd had a hard time dragging himself off the makeshift stake that had only narrowly missed his heart, and then hauling her out of the wreckage in a very weakened state.

He wasn't about to kill her now.

Not when he wanted to taste of her again

and again. No, he would keep this female around and keep her healthy. She was fast becoming an addiction.

He realized, belatedly, that he'd never healed as quickly as he had in the past twenty-four hours with her blood in his system. He'd taken her blood out of necessity before he could find a safe place for them to seek shelter. Luckily, she hadn't bled much in the crash, but her brain injury had looked serious. He would need more of her essence to heal himself before healing her more fully. Already, he had reduced the swelling in her skull somewhat with his healing gift. She would be much better, if not fully recovered, after a second session. But to do that, he must be stronger.

Her blood energized him. And her responsive body tripled the energy he derived from her blood. Her blood had been potent before, but now that she'd come so beautifully for him, his energy level peaked. He was near full strength. As she would be, as soon as he found the strength to tear himself away from her juicy neck and give her the healing she needed.

But she was so sweet!

With a groan, he backed off, using a light

zap of his healing touch through his tongue as he licked the sensitive skin of her neck. She squirmed deliciously under him, but he knew he had to finish her healing first, before satisfying other needs.

Settling the unaccustomed hunger for her blood—and her body—would come later.

"Are you all right?" He nuzzled her neck a moment longer.

"I'm..." She gasped as he moved upward to kiss her lips. "I'm okay. Please..."

"Please what?" He lifted to look down at her expression, which held a hint of dismay, a huge helping of bliss and a smattering of residual fear. "Please *please* you again? I'd be happy to, but it will have to wait until I can heal your wounds a bit more."

In the darkness he saw the faint elevation of color in her cheeks. It made him hard to realize that even after the blood he'd taken from her beautiful body, she could still blush. He'd always liked modest women— something that was becoming increasingly hard to find in this modern world.

"Heal me? So you're not... You're not going to kill me?" Her beautiful eyes were wide with apprehension and he didn't like her looking at him that way.

"No, sweetheart." He stroked her hair, trying to impart reassurance with a gentle touch. "I wouldn't have bothered carrying you from the wreckage if I intended you harm. I'm a healer. Even before I became...what I am...I had the gift of healing. I only want to use it to make you well. What comes after that is in the hands of fate."

"What are you?"

Atticus sighed. He should have expected the question. He'd left himself wide open for it, but he hadn't thought beyond the need to comfort this small mortal woman.

"I'm immortal."

"Like a vampire?" Fear clouded her words, but he also sensed fascination. It was a good sign.

"Some call us that, though it's not a term I prefer. There's too much incorrect mythology associated with the word and too much fear as well. We're mostly peaceful beings, only seeking to co-exist."

"But you feed on human blood, right?"

He nodded, sitting up by her side. The light in the cavern was dim, but he could see her plainly. He suspected she could make out his form as well, from the way her gaze tracked his movements, though without doubt her vision was less able to cope with the dark than his.

"As you experienced yourself, we do need blood to survive. Blood and sex. We are creatures of energy, and the psychic power released during orgasm is ambrosia to us."

"So that's why you made me…"

"Come? Yes, sweetheart." He liked teasing her, oddly enough, though he usually didn't waste much time conversing with his mortal prey. "You came beautifully for me and increased my strength. You helped heal me and I will do the same for you in return."

He wasn't a man who often indulged in the pleasures of the flesh. He had many gifts to bring prey to him. Clouding mortal minds so they never knew of his feeding from them had proved to be one of his most powerful abilities. He had often brought females to orgasm as he fed from them, because it usually doubled the potency of their blood, but he didn't take pleasure for himself. He hadn't even considered doing so in a very long time. Just one more thing to fall by the wayside as the malaise of his endless existence festered and grew.

But this small woman had ended all that.

With one look, she'd sparked a fire that brought him back to life. Back to passion. She fed his hunger like no other. He didn't regret the impulse that made him save her. He didn't regret living, though only the day before he had welcomed death. She gave him reason to go on, a flicker of hope in his increasingly dark world.

She might even be the One.

His breath caught at the enormity of the thought. He searched her pale features. She was beautiful to him, even covered with smudges of dirt and her hair in disarray. He knew she experienced more than a little pain from her head injury, but she seemed content, still a bit warm and fuzzy from the climax he'd given her. Strange pride filled him at having put that dreamy look in her eyes.

Each immortal searched for their One—the single person in the entire world who completed them. Most never found their mate. Many went insane and became true monsters. But a few, like him, walked the earth for centuries on end, searching.

The idea that he might have found her, just when he'd been ready to end it all, astounded him. He hardly dared believe. But there were signs...ancient signs that led him to believe that she might just be his One.

First, her blood was more potent than any he had ever had, and her orgasm fueled his own desire in a way he hadn't experienced in many decades. He wanted to come inside her to see if the rest of the legend could possibly be real.

Could they share their minds?

Could they truly become One?

Healing would have to come first, but he had to go slow. Brain injuries needed special care. He'd taken the risk of drinking from her and giving her pleasure because there was no way to restore his own health without her blood. As he'd absorbed her essence, his strength had returned and he'd been able to block the worst of her pain and make her focus on the good sensations he gave her. It had been a risk, but there had been no other way and he was confident in his ability to heal her completely, now that he was fired up with the life that ran so beautifully through her veins.

CHAPTER THREE

"How old are you?" Curiosity overcame Lissa's better judgment. The idea that she was sitting naked, in a dark cave with a friendly vampire was simply too weird.

"I've walked the earth far longer than you, sweetheart," he replied with a chuckle. From the sound of his voice and the vague shadows she could just make out, he'd moved away.

"My name is Lissa." She tried to sit, making it only to her elbow before her head started spinning.

"Lissa." The rumble of his voice cut off her next question. She'd been about to ask his name, but it didn't seem to matter when he was beside her, his warm breath wafting over her skin and his voice rumbling through every pore. "A beautiful name for a beautiful woman. Here." He supported her shoulders and took her hand, placing some kind of small basket in her grasp. Or was it a cup? She couldn't make out much in the murky darkness of the cave, but she could both hear and feel liquid sloshing around within the small receptacle she now held. "I collected some water for you. This cave has a little spring near the back that should be safe for you to drink."

"What is this?" She touched the rim of the cup, feeling branches and leaves.

He settled beside her. "I wove some twigs together and lined it with leaves. It's not entirely waterproof, but it works well enough. Drink, Lissa. You need fluids."

She found a smooth spot on the rim where leaves had been folded over the twigs and tried a sip. The water was cold and incredibly refreshing. She drank the whole cup, smacking her lips as she lowered the makeshift container.

A shock went through her system when he leaned down and licked her lips, turning the caress into a kiss that was sweeter than anything she'd ever tasted

"You are beautiful, Lissa, and you taste good enough to eat." His whispered words caressed her face as he lifted away, a millimeter at a time.

Her head swam as he let her go and her vision clouded. The man was potent, but she was still feeling the effects of being knocked around the interior of the shuttle bus as it careened down the mountain. He laid her back on the thin padding of their ruined clothes, and stroked her cheek with light, comforting motions.

"I'm sorry, sweet Lissa. You need to rest."

"Don't leave me." She clutched at his arm as he made to move away. She had no idea where the impulse came from, but she didn't want to be alone. In particular, she didn't want this compelling man—creature of the night though he was—to go far from her. She needed his warmth, his presence at her side. He made her feel safe, though just why she should feel safe with a vampire, she couldn't say. Logically, she should be trying to escape him, but logic had nothing to do with the terror in her heart at the thought of his leaving her.

"I won't. I promise you. But you need to rest more before I attempt the next phase of your healing. As do I. Healing takes something out of the healer and I was injured in the accident as well."

"Oh no." She hadn't truly understood before, her thought processes clouded by everything she'd had to deal with since waking. "Are you all right?"

"Don't worry for me, sweet Lissa." He brought her hand to his lips and kissed her knuckles with an old-world flair. "I'm much recovered since tasting of you. Just a few minutes rest will have me at full strength and ready to give some of that energy back to you. But I want to be sure to do this right. Brain injuries can be difficult. I want to make certain we're both ready when I attempt to heal you completely."

Silence descended as he settled beside her. He held her hand, offering warmth and comfort she wouldn't have believed possible from a vampire.

"I thought you guys were supposed to be cold."

He gave a long-suffering sigh. "The myths about my kind are seldom correct."

"Then what is true? I already know you drank my blood—unless I was hallucinating that part."

"No, you weren't hallucinating. Though I normally leave the mortals I drink from with no memory of the event. They don't tend to handle the idea as well as you have."

"I must've gotten my brains scrambled by the accident," she admitted. "I don't understand why I trust you, but I do. Maybe it's stupid of me to tell you that, but I can't see how my situation could be any worse."

"Oh, it could be worse, little one, but lucky for you, your trust—amazing as it is— is not misplaced this time. I want only to protect you. Of course, even if I were an ancient *Venifucus* killer, I might still tell you that, to keep you cooperative."

The irony in his voice comforted her. Something in her deepest mind liked him. Not only liked him, but trusted him. It was the same place the feelings of mixed dread and elation had come from when she'd been about to board the shuttle bus.

She understood the warning now. The dread was most likely a premonition of the accident and the death that would visit all those innocent souls in the vehicle. The elation might have something to do with her rescuer. From the first sight of his handsome face, she'd been drawn to him.

Destiny wasn't something she often tried to fight. She was just talented enough psychically to understand things sometimes happened as they were meant to happen. Fighting against fate only made life more difficult.

His words caught her attention, the niggling of her second sight alerting her to something important. Or perhaps it was something that would be important later. Either way, she trusted her abilities enough to investigate.

"What's that word? Veni-something?"

"*Venifucus.*" The foreign word rolled off his tongue, but a shiver of premonition set her nerves jangling. "It's an old word. A name for a group of killers who left this realm eons ago." He was quiet for a moment, as if reflecting. "I'm not sure why that popped into my mind now, when I haven't thought of them for centuries."

Lissa knew enough to tuck the information away for later consideration. Her gift sometimes guided her to learn strange tidbits that became useful months, sometimes years, later.

"Centuries?" The thought gave her pause as he sighed. One of his warm hands stroked her shoulder, offering comfort.

"I was born in what you would call the

Dark Ages, though to us, they were just hard times. My family owned a small vineyard, as I do today."

"You make wine? But...?" She didn't know how to ask him the questions running through her mind. A vampire businessman? It seemed too weird to contemplate.

"I can drink wine. In fact, it's a delicacy to my kind, though we can't ingest much else without consequences. But the fruit of the vine is our one last link to the sun. It heals us and invigorates us. I've always enjoyed the winemaking process and in one form or another, I've been involved in wine production since about the fourteen hundreds." He sounded as proud as any successful businessman talking about his career. "My main vineyard lies in the valley below. In fact, we're not too far from my land here. Perhaps tonight I can venture out and get some clothing and food for you. Or if you're well enough, you can come to my home and get cleaned up. We'll call the hotel from there and let them know you're all right."

"I was on my way to a conference, looking for a job. Guess that's out now, all things considered." She didn't want to think about her dwindling bank account or the bills that had been piling up.

"You won't make the conference, but try not to worry. I have a lot of business connections. Perhaps we can find you a job, once you're healed."

Tears gathered in the back of her eyes at this man's incredible kindness. Not only had he heroically dragged her from the wreckage and saved her life, but he was talking about helping her get her career back on track. He was almost too good to be true and under other circumstances, she probably would have been very wary, but she'd been drawn to him from the first. Fate, it seemed, had thrown them together, and for better or worse, her destiny was intertwined with his—at least for the foreseeable future.

Atticus lay beside her, attuned to her moods as he'd never been with any other being, mortal or immortal. It was as if he could sense her emotions, though he'd never had any kind of empathic abilities before.

She was a complex woman. Her surface thoughts were chaotic after the trauma she'd been through, but he sensed an inner core of strength he had seldom encountered in any being, and almost never in a female. She was remarkable in every way.

He could feel her fretting over her lack of a job. Atticus didn't want to frighten her by being too forward, but she had nothing to worry about. If necessary, he'd create a job for her—if she really wanted one. Although the longer he was in her presence, the more he thought seriously about keeping her. He had enough money to support an army. He could keep one small woman in style for the rest of her natural life.

But that was the sticking point. She was mortal. He'd never made a practice of keeping mortal pets around his home as some of his brethren did. It smacked of slavery to his mind and he didn't hold with that. For the first time, he was considering asking a woman to stay with him who knew full well what he was and what he'd want from her. There was no way he could keep her under his roof and not want to taste her blood again and again.

It was a momentous step.

He'd have to think carefully about the consequences before he broached the subject. There was also the improbable, but tantalizing idea that she could actually be his One. He'd find the answer to that question before he went any further, but he didn't dare get his hopes up too high. He'd searched the world over for centuries. He'd almost come to terms with the idea that he would never share his immortal life with one special woman. Almost. But there was a small part of him that still yearned for that impossible dream. Perhaps this woman was the answer to his quest. Perhaps.

But he had to heal her first, then take her, to be absolutely certain one way or the other.

Atticus leaned up on one elbow, looking down at her lovely face in the darkness.

"Don't fret, sweet. It will all work out. For now, let's concentrate on making you well, all right?"

Her expression lightened, much to his relief. "All right. I just wish everything would stop spinning." She chuckled and closed her eyes, likely unable to see much more than shadows in the dim cave.

"I can help with that." Gently, he placed his hands around the points of impact on her skull as he gathered his renewed strength. Using his healing gift, he directed pulses of energy to the places in her badly bruised head that were still injured. He'd done a lot of the repair work already, but the finer points had been beyond him the night before. He'd stabilized her, but left the finesse work until he was stronger.

Concentrating, he set to work. It took quite a while, but when he finally released her, she was healthy once more.

And ready for what he planned next.

"How does that feel? Is the headache any better?" His deep voice drifted down to her from above.

She felt so good with his hands on her face, in her hair. Her eyes had drifted shut of their own volition while he'd touched her, her unconscious mind trusting him in ways she'd never really trusted another being. Even with the few lovers she'd had in her life, she'd never fully let go and let them control her body or her responses. With this strange, startling man, giving over all her power was second nature.

Her body recognized him on some intrinsic level that she didn't bother to question. She knew from past experience with her psychic gift that some things defied logical explanation. Her uncharacteristic response to this imposing male creature was undoubtedly one of them.

Her eyes flickered open. She could see

31

him a little better in the dim light that filtered into their underground sanctuary from somewhere behind her. His form was less fuzzy than it had been. She took that as a good sign as she raised one hand to touch her head.

"The pain is gone. My head doesn't hurt anymore and I think my vision is clearer, though I still can't see much in this darkness. But it's better. I feel much better. Thank you."

"You're quite welcome, my dear." She could just make out his eyelids lowering as if he was fighting fatigue.

"Are you okay? I mean…" She tried to see his expression in the darkness. "I hope you didn't overtax yourself. Will you be all right?"

He brought her hand to his lips for a gentle salute. "You are sweet to think of my comfort, beautiful Lissa. It's true that healing takes a great deal of energy, but I'll be fine."

"Is there anything I can do?" She grew concerned by his quiet words, his restrained tone.

He paused before answering. "There is something you—we—could do to strengthen us both, my dear, but I hesitate to ask."

"What is it?" She tried to rise on one elbow, but he moved closer again, forcing her to remain beneath him.

"I told you I can gain strength from sexual release." His eyes actually sparkled. She could see them twinkle in the dim light. "I can pleasure you—and myself—if you'll allow it, and bring us both back to full strength."

CHAPTER FOUR

"You want to...uh...*be* with me?" Her hesitation stood between them as he gazed down at her. She wanted to be sure she understood him perfectly. It would be all too easy to build impossible dreams around a man like this.

"I want to make love to you, sweet Lissa. There is quite a difference." He leaned in, nibbling on her bare shoulder.

"But I'm not on anything." Her face flushed with embarrassment. "I mean..." she was at a loss for words.

"Never fear, sweetheart. You can't get pregnant with me. Not unless..." He didn't finish the thought, but she sensed wistfulness in his words.

"What?"

"The only way I could make you pregnant is if you were my one, true, destined mate,

which is highly unlikely. I've searched for
centuries and never found her." Silence
stretched before he continued. "You can't
catch anything from me. We don't suffer
from or carry mortal diseases. You're safe."

Lissa was uncomfortable with the
direction of the conversation, but he didn't
let up. If anything, he moved closer.

"I've pleasured many women in my years
but have not sought my own pleasure in a
very long time. I didn't want to. Not until I
met you."

"You don't have to lie to me." Hurt
seeped into her words regardless of her
desire to hide her feelings. They were too
close to the surface. This incredible situation
and incredible man were doing things to her
emotions that she couldn't control.

He drew back, his face hovering above
hers where she could see more of his
expression. His eyes were clear, gleaming
orbs in the darkness, the tight lines around
his mouth showing clearly how tense and
tired he was.

"I do not lie. When we first touched, I
knew there was something different about
you. You drew me, Lissa, unlike any woman
in many, many years. I wanted you from the

moment I saw you, though I'd planned only to track you down at the hotel, cloud your mind and drink of your essence. But now that I've tasted you, I doubt I could've stopped there. Had we not been in the wreck I would still have found you and wanted to bed you. Your warmth and energy are tantalizing to me."

"Really?" Her voice was small, her feelings unsure, but she was fascinated by the idea of what he'd have done if they hadn't been in a wreck. He might've come to her and she would have had no memory of this elegant, strong, incredible man.

All in all, she was glad now for the wreck, if only because he hadn't been able to cloud her mind. She wanted to remember every moment with this man, to hold against the years in the future. She was sure she would never meet another like him.

His very existence proved to her that magic was real—not only the magic of the vampire, but the magic of him. He was everything she had ever dreamed of in a man, and never dared hope for. She knew there was no future for them, but for this one moment out of time, she could experience what it was like to be held in his arms, to be made love to the way she'd dreamed of all her life. It was worth the risk to her heart, though she suspected it would be very easy to fall in love with him. But it was a chance she was willing to take.

Whenever he touched her, unearthly flames licked over her senses, warming her soul. Lissa didn't understand it at all, but reveled in the feel of his hands, his quiet strength. She wanted this dark stranger. She wanted him inside her with a passion unknown to her.

"Yes, sweet Lissa." His voice drifted over her. "I would have ravished you in the dark, given half a chance."

His words ignited a frenzy of need in her body. She could no more deny him than she could deny the fire racing through her veins. She reached for him, needy, yearning.

"Please," she said simply, suspecting he could see every nuance of her thought process in her expression. It was obvious now that he could see much better in the dark than she. It was yet another tidbit of memory about this experience she would file away to recall later, when he was gone from her life.

He bent, kissing the smile from her lips,

inflaming her with a fever she'd never known, but had always yearned for in her dreams. His fire licked over her senses as his tongue dueled with hers. His teeth were sharp, reminding her of the way he'd bitten her and made her come, but she wasn't frightened. Far from it.

"Your skin is like silk, sweet Lissa," he whispered against her skin as he moved down her body, placing nibbling kisses down across her collarbones and onto the swell of her breasts. His hands stroked lower, first circling her hips, then delving between her legs, urging her to spread them for his passage. Lissa was beyond shyness, beyond any thought of demur. This man aroused her passion unlike any other man before. She knew she was already slick and when his fingers encountered the evidence of her desire, he raised his head to stare into her eyes. He was so close, she could see the excited sparkle in his gaze, pinning her beneath him with the gentlest touch.

"Please..." she gasped. She wasn't sure what she was begging for exactly, but she knew he could provide it. He was the answer to all things at that moment.

"Yes, sweet Lissa. You're ready and I

can't wait. I have no finesse. Forgive me."
He slipped one finger into her channel. "But
I need to know." His words registered dimly
as he kissed her again, thrusting his tongue
inside her mouth the way she wanted him to
thrust himself inside *her*. The lascivious
thought made her squirm as that first finger
was joined by another, sliding in rhythm in
and out of her channel. She wanted him bad
and his stroking only made the yearning
worse.

"Please!" she cried out.

"Say yes. I need to hear it from your lips."

She could barely talk, let alone think.
He'd driven her passion higher, faster, than
she'd ever experienced. Yet, his patience was
impressive. He waited, even though it had to
be clear she was his for the taking. His hard
cock rubbed against the skin of her thigh as
he moved closer, bobbing, stroking and
driving her insane. She had to have him now,
but he waited for her permission.

He removed the fingers tormenting her,
moving over her so he could fit his hard
length into the space made for him. She tried
to move down onto him, but his strength
denied her. Her frustration level rose higher
and higher as she strained toward him.

Finally, she could take no more.

"Yes! Dammit, yes!" She panted against him. "Come into me now."

With an animalistic growl, he pushed forward, breaching the tightness of her body with a slow, firm, inward thrust.

Even in his passion, he moved carefully, lest he hurt her. He'd felt how tight she was with his fingers. He knew she'd have trouble taking him at first, but she'd adapt, and come to love his possession. He'd make her sing out in joy when she came around him, and he could hardly wait to bring her with him, over the edge into bliss.

But first, he had to get fully inside. He thrust shallowly, reveling in the feel of her passage. She was tight, but her maidenhead was absent. She'd had other men before him. With a wave of dominance, he was glad she'd have something to compare him with. This way, she'd know their joining was nothing ordinary.

No, this joining would be of epic proportions. He felt the heat rising already. Things were churning inside him in a way that was new to him and the boost to his energies coming from their joining spiked higher.

It was even better than the best he'd ever had. Stronger, more fulfilling and hotter than hell.

He let himself dare to hope that she might be the One. He didn't need the final sign that would come with climax, to know it in his heart. She was his One. He could feel it in his bones as he began to thrust deeper, keeping time with her cries of passion.

"Are you with me, sweetheart?"

He needed her to look at him, even though she could barely make him out in the darkness of the cave. But he needed to see her sparkling eyes as his body joined fully with hers this first time.

"I'm with you." Her words were faint gasps of air as she climbed ever higher with him.

"My name is Atticus," he told her, thrusting hard and deep, fully embedding himself as if he would never leave. "Say my name, Lissa. I need to hear it on your lips."

She panted. "Atticus." Her inner muscles clenched around him as she rose higher still. "Faster, Atticus. I need it harder." Her words were heated whispers of delight and yearning.

He complied with a groan of satisfaction,

seating himself deep. He pumped hard, reaching into her mind with his to know when and how she wanted him to thrust. But her thoughts were in perfect alignment with his and he noted the ease with which he accessed her mind as yet another sign that she was his One.

The thought brought him to a trembling precipice. She was right there with him. With a final push, he tumbled over the edge, his body spurting inside her as she screamed in ecstasy, clenching around him.

He hadn't come so hard in years, if ever. And she loved every minute of it. He could feel the satisfaction in her mind—a mirror of his.

Magnificent, joyous union. At last.

Pathways opened between their two souls, joining them together for all time. He realized with a blinding flash that he had full access to her memories now, as if they were his own. He wondered if she would have the same access to his mind. The thought gave him pause. Some of his memories were too grim to share with such a kind and gentle woman.

She was such a bright beacon of hope in his otherwise dark world. He didn't want to subject her to his memories, including centuries of living in a world that had been sometimes harsh, and even inhuman. He doubted she could accept the more sinister parts of his long existence.

"Don't think that, Atticus." She shocked him with her words as she stroked his chest with trembling fingers. "There is no part of you that I couldn't accept."

"Then you share my mind?" His heart opened in joy at the thought. He'd found her at last. Joined in mind, they were truly One.

"How could I not? I was more than a little psychic even before the wreck. I knew there was something different about you the moment you stepped on my foot."

He chuckled and moved his heavy weight off her, settling at her side.

"Psychic?" He stroked her shoulder as he contemplated the ramifications. He hadn't realized she had any kind of extrasensory abilities, but he could read now, the way her gift had helped her in the past. His new mate was full of surprises that he would spend the rest of their years discovering.

"It runs in my family. But I've never experienced anything like what just happened, or what I'm learning now, seeing inside your memories. It's amazing. And a bit overwhelming." Softened with awe, her voice washed over him.

"Do you understand what you see in my memories? Do you understand that you are my One? My *raison d'etre*? My everything?" Anxiety filled him as he waited for her all-important reply.

She rose to lean over him this time, stroking his bristly cheek with reassurance. "When we climaxed together, it all came to me in a blinding rush. I'll admit, there are some things I'll have to think through and sort out, but the most important thing is that my heart recognized you, Atticus. Not only am I your One, but you're mine." She leaned down to kiss his lips sweetly. "And I want you to bring me over."

He sucked in a breath of shock. "Are you sure?"

If she drank his blood, she would become immortal too. They would share eternity—together.

He'd planned to talk her into it in time. It was a big change for a human, and he hadn't wanted to push. Now she'd broadsided him with her decision and her delighted chuckle told him as clearly as the mischievous thoughts in her mind that she enjoyed it.

"Yes, I'm sure, Atticus. I love you."

The vacant place in his soul suddenly filled with her blindingly bright light.

The most sacred quest of his long lifetime had ended, and now he could get on with living and enjoying his immortal existence with a woman he loved by his side.

"I love you, Lissa. And I always will."

She lightened his heart as he pulled her over him. With a sharp thrust, he brought them together once more, both ready for more. Sharing minds made all aspects of life better, they discovered as his cock drove home where it belonged, right up inside her, as far as nature allowed. She squirmed in delight. Her body knew his. It recognized its other half.

It was a slow joining, a lazy thrust and return that they both wanted to draw out.

"When you make me a vampire, will I have to suck other people's blood?" She didn't sound too thrilled with the idea, and he easily read the aversion to touching other men in her mind, which pleased him greatly.

"Now that we are One, you need only drink my blood. Our love and our blood will sustain us both now."

"So no more biting the necks of women you don't know?"

He grinned as he brought her higher with a deep thrust. "No, love. Just you. And I'll bite," he pulled her down so her heavy breasts were inches away from his mouth, "only you. All of you. From here to forever." He reached up with his tongue and licked her nipples, pulling each deep into his mouth in turn, as she moaned above him.

She began to ride him, her breath hissing out as her pleasure rose, and he reveled in the wicked thoughts in her mind. His girl liked it a little kinky, it seemed. They would have centuries together—Lady willing—to explore all their shared desires. Atticus liked the wicked thoughts in her mind that marched so well with his own tastes. That they were compatible in this way was only more proof that she had been made just for him.

"You're a naughty girl, aren't you?" He liked the way Lissa gasped, her skin heating. He knew she was both embarrassed and enthralled by the idea of playing sexy games with him. "Answer me, sweetheart." A tinge of dominance filled his tone and he felt her clench around him. No doubt about it. She liked it.

"Yes, Atticus. I've been bad."

"Very bad," he agreed with a satisfied smile. They were definitely both on the same page. "Now what do we do with bad girls?" He let the words draw out as he slowed his upward thrusts, holding her on a knife's edge of pleasure. She moaned and he sensed words were beyond her at this point. "Do you want to feel the force of my hand on this pretty ass, sweetheart? Is that what you want? Do you want a spanking?"

Her eyes closed as she clenched and threw her head back. "Yes!"

That's all he needed to hear. Atticus swatted her ass and urged her to ride him faster. She began to whimper and moan on every deep thrust and every hard spank. Atticus tongued her nipples then grazed his fangs over the soft flesh on the side of one full breast, drawing just a bit of blood that he greedily lapped up.

She loved it. He read the exciting flash of sexy pain that thrilled her, and the resulting pleasure as he stroked his tongue over her soft skin in her chaotic thoughts. He smacked her ass then moved one hand around to search out her little clit.

Unerringly, he grasped the tiny button, squeezing hard and making her come with a delicious shout that echoed through the dark cavern.

He followed her into madness as he shot his seed deep inside his mate.

His One and only.

CHAPTER FIVE

By nightfall, they were both back to full strength, though Lissa knew she would bear some black and blue bruises from the accident for the next few days. Atticus had discussed their next move with her and they'd decided to leave some evidence of her adventure for the human authorities to see. They would, no doubt, have been searching for her since the wreck that had claimed so many lives. Luckily, no one but the driver had known Atticus was on the shuttle bus, since his decision to go up to the resort had been a last minute thing.

As a result, they decided to placate the authorities with a story that made some sense, though it was admittedly sketchy. They arrived at Atticus's home just after sunset. To say it was a mansion was an understatement. The European-styled villa was set in the midst of a picturesque vineyard and both the house and manicured landscape took her breath away.

Opening the grand door, Atticus whisked her into his arms and carried her over the threshold. It was a romantic, old world gesture that brought tears to her eyes.

"Welcome home, love." He paused to kiss her, keeping her in his arms as he kicked the door shut and carried her into a spacious living room.

The kiss grew bolder as he lowered her to a soft, wide couch. She could feel the conflict inside him. He wanted to call the authorities on one hand, to begin the process of making her completely well. On the other hand, he shared the raging desire burning in her own blood to make love here and now— to claim her without further delay.

"Yes, Atticus. Yes." She stroked his skin, taking the decision out of his hands. "Make love to me."

"Are you certain?" He pulled back only slightly. "I don't want to hurt you. I hated to leave even one small bruise on your skin when I could easily have healed them all."

"You could never hurt me," she reassured him. "And we needed to leave some of the bruises to show the nice ambulance men," she teased with a coy smile. "But I want you now, Atticus. I don't want to have to wait until they let me out of the hospital. I can't go two minutes without wanting you. I'm addicted to you." She laughed to ease his strain, cupping his cheek and looking deep into his mesmerizing eyes.

"You do the same to me, Lissa, and it's an addiction I pray never to quit." He swooped in for a devastating kiss, aligning his body with hers on the plush sofa. "I can't resist you. But we do this my way. I don't want you in any pain whatsoever."

"Whatever you say... Master." She gave him a saucy smile as she read his need for domination in their shared minds. She was getting better at reading him the more they were together, though the idea that they were One still boggled her mind.

He growled and nipped her neck playfully, then worked his way down her body. They were both naked and he took full advantage, pausing to lick one pointy nipple into his mouth, then the other until she was writhing on the soft fabric.

"Please..." she moaned in need.

"Don't move." Atticus left her sensitive

breasts, nipping the swell of her tummy next as he worked his way downward. Strong hands pushed her thighs apart until one foot rested over the back of the sofa, the other on the floor. Then his mouth was on her, sucking her, his tongue stroking with flickering little licks that set her on fire.

Her passion rose like a skyrocket, bursting into a little explosion even as he pushed one long finger into the slick heat that was more than ready for deeper invasion.

"Atticus!" He rode her through the tiny storm, letting the waves break only to build again, stronger than before. She could feel him holding back, letting her pleasure override his own through their bond, and she loved him for it. He was so afraid he might inadvertently hurt her. The care he showed her was a beautiful thing and she was humbled by it, but she wanted him. She didn't want to wait any longer for his possession.

Atticus growled as he sat up. "This isn't going to work." He ran one hand raggedly through his hair. The gesture was endearing considering his frustration was all because of his care for her. Lissa followed him, crawling over him until she was seated on his lap. She'd never been so aggressive in lovemaking before, but she knew he liked it. He was probably as surprised as she was by her actions, but definitely fired up as she straddled his straining erection.

"I know you wanted to do this your way, but I like my way better." She stroked his cheek with hers, rubbing against him like a cat. She felt so sexy in that moment, it was a wonder she didn't purr. The silly thought brought a smile to her lips as she licked over his firm jaw and down to his neck. Two could play the neck nibbling game, though her teeth were admittedly not up to the task the way his were. Still, the sensation of her blunt teeth over his skin seemed to inflame him.

"Harder," he urged her, when she bit down on the muscle where his neck met his strong shoulder. She obliged, noting the little dents her teeth made in his skin as she pulled back.

"I think I'm going to love biting you after you change me."

He stilled. "You really want that? You'll join me in my darkness?"

"I'll join you in the dark, in candlelight, in

the ocean, in an airplane. Anywhere you are, I'll be there." She gave him a shy look from under her eyelashes, playing with him. "If you want me."

"If I want you?" He growled and flipped her over his legs, ass up. He swatted her butt and made her squeal with pleasure. "Woman! How could you doubt it? I'll gladly join the mile high club with you. I have a friend with a very nice jet he'd be willing to loan us. Just name the date."

She giggled as he rubbed her stinging bottom, then spanked her again.

"Are you laughing at me, Lissa?" His mock outrage made her laugh harder as her breathing sped. His hand came down in sharp slaps against the fleshy part of her ass, driving her higher.

She loved it. She didn't understand it. She'd never been spanked by any man before Atticus, but with him, it just felt right...and really, really exciting.

"I asked you a question, wench."

She had to think back to remember what he'd been saying as his hand landed a few more times. She was more than hot at this point. She was steaming and ready for anything he could give her.

"Um…"

"What was that? I asked you if you were laughing at me, sweetheart."

"No. No, I'm not laughing at you." She gasped as his fingers began to travel the crack of her ass, dipping within the slick heart of her to tickle and tease, making her yearn for more. "Please, Atticus! I need you now."

"Are you sure? Do you think you've been a good girl? Do you deserve a treat?"

She could have slapped him when he laughed, but she knew it was all in good fun. Still, she wasn't feeling very humorous at the moment. No, at the moment, she needed him inside her. She needed him. Period.

He toyed with her, his fingers driving her crazy—a poor substitute for what she really wanted. She wiggled and moaned, but he was merciless.

"Atticus… Please."

He finally took pity on her, lifting her up and placing her on her back, positioning her like a rag doll. He was so strong, he took her breath away. Yet he was as gentle with her as if he handled the most delicate crystal. He paused above her, his hard cock so close to where she wanted it most, but he made her look into his eyes as he braced himself above her on his elbows.

"I love you, Lissa."

Her heart melted. "I love you too." Her pledge was spoken in a whisper, stronger for its emotional depth. She felt their words ringing through the bond they shared, making it stronger. "Come to me, Atticus. I need you."

"I'll always need you," he confirmed as he took her lips and claimed her body with one smooth move. He pushed inside her, sliding easily in the thick arousal he'd caused. She moaned as she felt him slide all the way home. Where he belonged.

CHAPTER SIX

The ride was only just beginning. Atticus paused for just a moment as he kissed her long and deep, but soon he was thrusting in long sweeps, almost pulling out only to plunge home again, over and over. She cried out and wriggled under him as his motions drew her higher. He knew just how to move to give her the most pleasure.

That this spectacular man was all hers only heightened her passion. She'd known him such a short time, but time meant little to something as powerful as their love. Their joined souls meant they knew the core of each other's personality without even trying. They were truly One.

She felt his raging desire as a reflection of her own as he drove them both faster and higher. She clutched at his shoulders as he lowered his head, stroking his tongue over

her neck as the sharp points of his fangs
dropped to zing her with little pinpricks of
unexpected pleasure before sinking deep into
her jugular.

The moment he struck, her orgasm began
and it went on and on while he sucked at the
sensitive skin of her neck. She felt him come
as he pulled her essence into himself, bathing
her in a wash of his pleasure. Lissa cried out
at the wonder of their shared souls, their
shared passion, their shared bodies. She
loved this man more than anyone or
anything she'd ever known and would for
the rest of their days.

Atticus withdrew his teeth from her skin
and licked over the wounds, sparking closure
of her wounds so there was no mark left to
mar her skin or betray his predilection for
biting her. She was too sated to do more
than follow when he lifted her over his body,
changing their position so she'd be more
comfortable as her eyes closed and sleep
overtook her.

"I've been granted a miracle, Lissa. I love
you more than life and I'll never let you go.
Never." He kissed her temple as he settled
her over his heart.

The last thing she heard as she drifted off

was his words of love. She slept against her mate with a smile curving her lips.

Much later, Atticus placed calls to both the resort and the police, spinning a tale about how Lissa had just shown up on his doorstep out of the blue. Atticus brought her to the bedroom he kept above ground and gave her some of his clothes to wear. She had just enough time to clean up while an ambulance was summoned. His shirt was too large for her as she emerged from the bathroom of the master suite and she looked adorable in it.

"They'll be here soon, my love. Undoubtedly, they'll want you to go to the hospital, maybe even keep you there until tomorrow." He took her hand, drawing her down to sit beside him on the downy bed. "I regret I cannot go with you, but it wouldn't make much sense to the authorities. I don't want to raise any sort of suspicion. Plus, it's bound to take a while for them to reassure themselves that you're all right. Likely they won't let me be near you while they run their tests and it could take all night." He shrugged. "The police will likely want to take my statement and check my land, so I'll need to be here to show them around. I could cloud their minds, of course, and the people at the hospital, but crowds are tricky. If I miss even one mind, I could be putting us both in danger of discovery. It's safer for me to remain here, all things considered. Being caught out in the sun is dangerous for my kind, as it will be for you once you are turned."

She smiled, assuring him of her love. "I'll enjoy the sun for a few days yet, but I won't miss it too much, if I can have you in return."

"You'll always have me, my love." He drew her knuckles to his lips in a gentle kiss. "Once you square things away with the hotel, I want you to come back to me. Tomorrow night, I want you to lie beside me, here, in our home."

"I want the same thing, Atticus. I'll get my stuff from the hotel and be knocking on your door right as the sun goes down."

He drew away to reach into his trouser pocket, producing a set of keys as they both stood. "You don't ever have to knock. What's mine is yours. This is your house too. You will make it a home as it has never been…until now." He pressed the ring of keys into her palm, closing her fingers

around the cold metal while her eyes filled
with tears.

She hugged him close, burying her face
against his chest. He held her for long
moments, until at last, he heard the buzzer
that indicated a vehicle was at the gate
leading to his estate.

"They're here."

"I know." She pulled away with a sad
expression on her lovely face. "But I don't
want to leave you."

"I will be near, Lissa. Wherever you go,
from now until eternity, all you have to do is
reach out with your mind and I'll be there.
We are One. In time, we'll learn how to
manage the joining better, but for now, just
think of me and I will be with you."

"Same goes for me, Atticus."

She drew back and they walked from the
bedroom, down a long hall and into the
main area of the house. Atticus flicked a
button on the way, releasing the gate so the
authorities could make their way up the
drive. They'd have to act like mere
acquaintances while the humans sniffed
around their home. Atticus had lived long
enough to know when the wiser course of
action was to play by human rules and this

was one of those times.

His new mate was human and had family and friends. They had to be careful how they managed her conversion so she could keep her human contacts for at least the length of her normal lifespan. After sufficient years had passed, they could reinvent themselves, as Atticus had done many times in the past. It was tricky to manage turning a human without cutting them off from all previous ties, but for Lissa, he would do anything. She deserved to keep her friends and family in her life and he wouldn't make her chose between them and him—if a true mate really had a choice. He knew full well, she didn't. Neither did he. They were destined for each other.

The police car came into view and Atticus went to meet them at the door. He paused before opening the portal, turning to look at her as she climbed under a blanket he'd spread on the wide couch.

"I love you more than I can ever express."

Her eyes filled again as her gaze met his. "Me too, Atticus." She sniffed, wiping her eyes with the back of one hand as she pulled the cover up to her chin. "Let's get this over with. The sooner I leave, the sooner I can return...to you."

"Atticus?"

"Here, my love." His deep voice purred through their shared minds. *"How are you holding up?"*

"They've got me in a private room. Things have quieted down a bit, but I had a few X-rays, plus a team of doctors checking me over in the emergency room. I think they're satisfied that I'm okay. As you suspected, they admitted me for the night. A nurse is supposed to wake me up every hour to check my eyes or something."

"They're probably concerned about the bump on your head. Does it hurt?"

"Not much. But you were right to leave a little bit of the damage from the crash. They're already marveling over how well I came through the wreck that killed everybody else."

"I'm sorry I had to leave a single mark on your beautiful body, but we have to be careful if you want to continue to live your current life."

"I appreciate all the thought and effort you've put into this, Atticus. I love my family and friends, but I love you more, especially for going out of your way to preserve my relationships with them. You're a special, amazing man and I can't believe you're in my life."

"*Same here, my love. And of course we need your family and friends, otherwise who will we invite to our wedding?*"

She paused, the flavor of her shock, delight and awe coming through loud and clear. "*You want to marry me?*"

"*Oh, yes. A wedding like you've always dreamed of, Lissa. With all the trimmings, including a big bridal party. I guess I'll have to come up with groomsmen to balance out your old college friends, eh?*" His chuckle sounded through their minds. "*But we'll have to have an evening wedding, of course.*"

"*I can't believe it.*"

"*Believe it, my love. I never thought to marry, and in the eyes of my people, we are already mated, but I know from your thoughts how important this is to you. I want you to have the ceremony and the reception of your dreams. That is, if you'll consent to be my wife. Sorry, I should have asked that first. Will you marry me, Lissa, and make me the happiest of men?*"

"*Yes! Yes, I'd be delighted to marry you, Atticus. I love you.*"

"*Hold that thought, love, for this evening. Dawn approaches and I must seek shelter for the day. Will you be all right today?*"

"*I'll be fine. They let me call my friend Jena.*"

64

She's a doctor. She should be here any minute, though she's not on staff at this hospital. She'll gather the rest of the group and they'll take good care of me. I'll get my things from the hotel and be at your place as soon as I can ditch my friends."

"Our place, Lissa. This vineyard is your home now too. Or we could move someplace else if you want. I'll live anywhere, as long as you're there."

"I know how much you love the vineyard, Atticus. That you'd be willing to give it up for me means a lot, but there's no need. The place is a dream. The house is lovely and the grounds are gorgeous. I'll be happy living there...with you."

"Good. Then hurry home, love. I'll be awaiting your return."

Jena entered Lissa's hospital room shortly after dawn, waking Lissa with her presence. Not long after Jena assured herself that Lissa really would be all right, their friend Kelly arrived with a change of clothes for when the doctors sprung Lissa later that morning. As Lissa had predicted, the troops were rallied and her friends circled around her, taking turns sitting with her and talking until the doctors let her go with a few words of instruction and a bottle of pain relievers.

Over their objections, Lissa had her friends take her first to the resort to collect her bags, which had been sent ahead. That accomplished, they took her home and stayed for lunch. Lissa laid the groundwork for her new relationship with Atticus by telling them of her plan to visit the man who'd rescued her, to return his shirt.

"Should you be driving after that knock on the skull?" Kelly wanted to know.

"The doctors said I'm fine, right, Jena?" Lissa turned her gaze on the doctor and Jena had to admit she was right. "Besides, I'm just going to drop off the shirt he let me use. Believe me, if you'd seen this man, you'd want to do the same."

"He's that good looking?" Jena asked as she poured tea for them all in Lissa's small kitchen.

"Better," Lissa said with a grin. "His name is Atticus Maxwell and he has lovely, mysterious eyes."

"Maxwell? *The* Atticus Maxwell who owns the most exclusive winery in the entire valley? They say he's a bit of a recluse, and eccentric too, though he bottles some of the best wine in the country—maybe even the world. It's won all kinds of awards," Kelly said with surprise widening her eyes. "Honey, he's one of the richest men in the valley. You showed up on *his* doorstep?"

"I didn't know whose house it was. It was just the first one I saw after walking away from the accident in a daze."

"You were very lucky, Lissa. And blessed. Somebody upstairs was watching over you." Jena's voice dropped to a hushed whisper. "I'm so glad you're okay."

A group hug followed and soon after, Lissa was able to usher her friends out the door of her apartment with promises to call the next day, or sooner, if she needed anything. Lissa set about packing her belongings, but only a few. She couldn't do anything too obvious yet. Atticus had cautioned her that they had to move slowly. But she filled a suitcase with clothes and shoes, taking a few mementoes that she wanted to have with her at his house. She watered her plants and closed up the apartment so it would be okay for a few days. It was unlikely she'd be back anytime soon. She wanted to spend every moment with Atticus and she knew he felt the same.

She threw the suitcase into the trunk of her car and headed out of town toward Atticus's place in the valley, about an hour away. He'd given her the keys and codes for the alarm system and gate. She didn't feel like a visitor or trespasser when she let herself into the big house. Instead, she felt very much as if she were coming home.

Lissa made dinner for herself in the sparkling clean kitchen. Atticus had a few canned goods and packaged foods in his cupboards, though she knew he didn't need to eat. Like many things about the giant house, it was stocked for the occasional mortal guest and designed to give Atticus every appearance of normalcy. His kind lived in secret and had for centuries. Atticus had explained earlier about the lengths he'd gone to give every appearance of being a normal man and there was no doubt he'd become very good at putting up a façade of mortality.

The kitchen was a dream—big and airy with every modern convenience—as was the rest of the house. She loved the Mission style furniture and earth tones that dominated most of the décor. She gave herself a tour of the above-ground rooms, pleased to find an art studio, a small home gym and a very busy-looking office. He found her there, while she was perusing his calendar, which was lying open on the desk.

She sensed him even before his muscular

arm snaked around her waist from behind, drawing her back against his hard chest. Warm lips traced the skin under her ear with just a hint of pointed teeth scraping against her, making her hotter than she'd ever been for any other man.

CHAPTER SEVEN

"Good morrow, my love." His deep voice sounded near her ear, sending shivers down her spine.

"Atticus." His name was a sigh of pleasure as he cupped one of her breasts, tugging and exciting her every nerve.

"I love to hear you say my name just that way." His warm chuckle skittered along her senses as he turned her in his arms. "Waking up to you in our home is a miracle, Lissa. One I never thought I would experience. I feel as if heaven is smiling on me for the first time in many long years."

The kiss they shared then was one of coming home, of undreamed of love, of safety and hope. Lissa didn't know how much time had passed when Atticus finally released her lips, but her head was spinning and she had to hold on to him for balance.

He'd made her dizzy with just his kiss.

"How do you like the house?" He moved further back, once he seemed sure she was steady on her feet. "I sensed your pleasure as you toured earlier, but as we're new to this joining, I thought we'd start slowly."

"How so?" She perched on the edge of his desk, since he seemed to want to talk.

"I have a lot more experience traipsing through people's minds than you, my dear." He gave her a sly smile. "I thought it best to give each other a little room to interact as any normal mortal couple would...in the beginning at least...when we're not making love. When I'm inside your body, I can't help but want to be in your mind as well."

Lissa remembered the way they'd joined the night before and shivered. There was nothing that could compare with the way they'd shared minds and bodies in the ultimate pleasure.

"I agree." She tried to smile, but her mouth was dry from the heat of her memories. "And I'll admit it's hard to get used to the idea of sharing our minds. I'm a little psychic, but I've only ever gotten the odd premonition here and there. I've never been able to read someone's thoughts, though it was rumored my grandmother could."

"Really?" Atticus seemed intrigued. "She must have been an amazing woman. Even without trying to enter your mind, I can feel the love and respect you have for her. Keeping the connection partially blocked will help us when we need to act normally in the company of mortals. Your friends, for example. At some point, I'll need to meet them."

Lissa laughed, thinking how her buddies would drool over Atticus. It wouldn't be too hard to convince them she'd fallen head over heels for the man in such a short amount of time.

"Give it a week or two. I have a standing dinner with the group a week from Wednesday. We get together every month to share gossip. I'll start getting them used to the idea that we're an item then."

"I see you've been giving this some thought as well." Atticus's approval washed over her senses. She'd never been all that empathic before, but she could feel his emotions, even if she wasn't directly reading his thoughts. "As for my friends," he lifted the calendar from the desk, "you'll meet one tonight. I've asked the Master to come meet you, since it's such a rare occurrence that one of us finds his mate. Marc and I have been friends a long time. You'll like him."

"You really call him Master?"

"Sometimes. It is his title, since he rules the bloodletters in this region. I'm in the hierarchy as well. I'm his second, actually. We have a small circle of friends, all of whom rank highly in the supernatural hierarchy hereabouts, but Marc is our leader. Hence the title of Master. But he's a good man. Not at all lord-of-the-manor. You'll see. I think you'll like him. He's got a wickedly sharp sense of humor."

She felt the genuine affection Atticus had for the other man and was intrigued. There was a devilish sparkle in his eye when he spoke of this "Master" that boded well. If Atticus liked him, chances were, she would too. They were aligned like that. Perhaps because they were mates.

Lissa felt cheated that they didn't have time to make love before Marc arrived, but as Atticus told her, it was better to get the formalities out of the way before they got too distracted. They would spend the rest of the night caught up in each other, she knew.

And Atticus was talking in terms of centuries together, which still overwhelmed her. They would have time.

Marc LaTour was handsome as sin and sharp as a tack. He greeted Atticus with a backslapping hug and then turned his arresting, assessing gaze on Lissa. She wanted to squirm under his inspection until she saw the very real awe in his expression. He seemed genuinely happy for Atticus and at the same time a little afraid of her. That dichotomy made her want to put him at ease.

Atticus poured wine for them all and Marc raised a toast to them. "I'm happy for you both," Marc said, sitting at ease in the cozy living room. "Between us, Lissa, I was growing concerned for my friend Atticus. He took chances he shouldn't have in recent years. Hopefully with you here, he'll be more careful. I value his friendship."

"As I value yours, my friend." Atticus tipped his wineglass in Marc's direction. "But please don't frighten my mate. All that matters now is that she *is* here and we are together. What came before matters not."

Lissa placed her hand over his, drawing his attention. "What came before made you what you are, Atticus, and I love every part of you. But you can rest assured," she transferred her attention to Marc, "there will be no more taking chances with his life. That carelessness is over."

She could see hints of the things he'd allowed to happen, the desolation in his life that led him to that shuttle bus and to the brink of death. Even with their connection moderated by his incredible psychic control, she knew he'd been near the end of his rope, but now that they'd found each other, his entire outlook had taken a radical turn.

"And glad I am to hear it." Marc stood, helping himself to a second glass of wine from the sideboard, clearly at home in Atticus's house. "But I have some news I must impart that makes it even more critical. I hesitate to say this in front of you, Lissa, for I don't mean to worry you, but as new mates, I've heard there's no way to really keep you from knowing what he knows, so…" Marc shrugged elegantly. Everything about the man was both devilish and suave.

Atticus sat forward. "What is it?"

"Ian looked over the accident site and the vehicle wreckage at my request. When he reported back at sunset, I went over there myself before coming here. Atticus, that was no accident, though the mortals will no doubt rule it as such. There was the faint scent of magic around the vehicle. I have no doubt it was tampered with."

"What flavor of magic? *Were*? Mortal? Fey? Or something else?" The rigidity in Atticus's spine and his narrow-eyed gaze alerted Lissa to the seriousness of the situation. She felt a hint of disbelief at their casual use of the term "magic", but then, she hadn't believed in vampires until a day ago either.

"It was something very old, indeed." Marc's eyes took on a faraway cast as he seemed to search for an answer. "It felt fey, but not quite. And ancient. It's something just tickling my memory, but I'm not altogether certain I've ever run across this particular kind of thing before. It's damned odd, to say the least. Ian's organizing surveillance in case the magic-user returns to the scene of the crime."

"Who were they targeting? Do you have any idea?"

"That's the hard part. The magic wasn't attuned to our kind, but neither was it attuned to any particular mortal that either Ian or I could discern. Plus we were working with only traces. Whoever cast the spell was skilled. Very skilled indeed."

"Nobody knew I was on that bus. It was a last minute decision on my part to go up to the resort. There were only a few other passengers—all mortal. Love," Atticus turned to Lissa, "you said you felt something as you boarded. Tell Marc what you felt. It might help solve this puzzle."

Lissa put her wineglass on the low table. "If you like." She turned to Marc and tried to put into words the feelings of dread that had hit her when she set foot on that shuttle bus. "There was a strong urge not to board, but it was generalized. I couldn't be sure, and the moment I saw Atticus, he intrigued me. Distracted me really." She sent Atticus a soft, teasing smile. "From him, I felt a different kind of energy—like I had just met my fate." Atticus squeezed her hand in encouragement. "The two instincts were in conflict, but my desire to follow Atticus was stronger than the feelings of dread."

"Thank heaven for that," Marc said with feeling that surprised her. "If you hadn't been on board and survived the crash, I doubt my good friend would still be among the living. No," he held up a hand to stall

Atticus's response, "don't object. I've sensed what was in your heart for months, brother. Without your One, you were nearly lost to us. Fate plays a bigger hand than we know. You were on that shuttle bus for a reason, Lissa, though you knew it was dangerous, you boarded anyway. That is significant."

"You think so?" The idea was startling to her, but it felt right.

"I do. I also think, until we know more about who and what caused the crash, you both need to be careful. It's unclear who the target was, but that wreck was no accident and quite a few innocents paid the price."

Lissa was struck with renewed sadness at the reminder of the loss of life. That she'd survived when everyone else died was nothing less than a miracle. A miracle named Atticus. And if Marc was to be believed, if she'd succumbed to her injuries, Atticus would have had no reason to save himself. They would both be dead.

The idea that someone deliberately caused the wreck by magical means was nearly overwhelming, but she'd been exposed to a number of strange happenings in her life. The existence of vampires was only the latest—and admittedly most astounding—of many odd things she'd seen. The idea that magic was real was somewhat easier to accept, given her recent experiences.

"You think whoever did that might have meant it for one of us?" Lissa's eyes widened at the thought. "I don't have any enemies that I'm aware of. Particularly not of the magical kind."

"I'm sorry, my dear, but you yourself said you were psychic. Certain beings would have been able to sense your power and some might even target you because of it. The supernatural world is a more brutal place than your mortal one sometimes. We try to preserve a delicate balance between those of us who would leave humanity to their own devices and those who would seek to dominate and even enslave them. And there are even a few groups of mortals who are aware of certain aspects of the supernatural world and seek to eradicate it. If someone knew of your abilities, you could very easily have been the target of the magical tampering."

Lissa held one palm over her racing heart. "I can't believe it."

Atticus squeezed her other hand, turning

toward her on the couch. "But you must, my love. You must believe that the threat could be to either of us and act accordingly. For starters, I want you to move in here. We'll go over to your apartment together and retrieve your things."

"But not tonight." Marc interrupted Atticus and stood to leave. "Ian is coordinating surveillance on Lissa's apartment and a few other places. I want to know who the target of the wreck was and why. Tipping our hand too early might cause them to scurry away. If one of you is still being targeted, we'll find out. The vineyard is well protected, but Lissa's place is not. It makes sense for you to stay here then, milady, though it might seem odd to your mortal friends. You'll have to inform them of a whirlwind romance and perhaps an impulsive wedding can be planned? You two can decide how to best handle that, but leave the dangerous part to me."

"I hardly know what to say." Lissa was at a loss. Marc was indeed a powerful man with a dominant way that she'd never encountered. Atticus was the strongest man she'd ever met. Before meeting him, she'd never dreamed the kind of man she fantasized about even existed. Atticus was perfect for her, but Marc...he was every bit as handsome, commanding and powerful as her new mate, though without the soft side that tempered her lover. He was formidable.

"Stay with your mate and be happy, milady. Let me handle the threat—if there is, indeed, any. We may come to find that another was the target and now that he or she is dead, the threat may vanish. Either way, it is far better to be safe than sorry."

Atticus rose and stretched his hand out for a brotherly shake. "I can't thank you enough, Marc. Lissa's safety is the most important thing in the world to me."

Marc nodded once. "Understandable. Even admirable. I envy you, my friend, and I aim to see that nothing threatens your future happiness. I'll be in touch when I know more. For now, rest here and stay safe."

They saw Marc to the door and Lissa was impressed by the low-slung, shiny black sports car he drove. That car had to cost more than ten years of rent on her apartment in the city and it purred like a big cat. These men—these vampires—were wealthy sons of guns.

CHAPTER EIGHT

Atticus locked up the house, arming the security systems and making certain all was as safe as he could make it. They had hours until sunrise and he wanted to spend many of them making love to his new mate. But before they let passion carry them away, they had some planning to do.

He led her toward the indoor pool housed on the back side of the house. It had a glass roof that he could open to the night sky in warm weather. The pool was surrounded by lush, tropical plants and had a small waterfall to make it look and feel like a naturally occurring grotto in some exotic destination.

"This is gorgeous at night. I saw it earlier today, but it's even more beautiful now." Lissa moved toward one of the large bird of paradise plants and stroked its leaves as she gazed out over the water.

"I'm glad you like it. I spend a lot of time out here, stargazing and contemplating the infinite." He moved to the small bar and poured two glasses of deep red wine, brought them toward the plush lounge chairs nearby. She sat and accepted one of the glasses, before he took the space next to her on the wide chaise. "Now, of course, I can sit out here and ponder you."

She laughed and sipped at the wine, smiling at him over the rim of the crystal glass. He wanted to make love to her right then and there, but they had a few things left to discuss first. He could wait. But not too long.

He put one arm around her as they leaned against the low back of the long chair, putting their feet up. He'd never been so comfortable in his entire existence.

"Do you think your friends will accept that I swept you off your feet so quickly?" Atticus had seen the close relationship Lissa had with the small group of women she'd befriended in college while sifting through her memories during their initial joining. He kept the mental block between their minds in place for now, because he knew it was more comfortable for her to learn him slowly—and they truly had eternity to do so. He'd savor this time of learning her as she got used to him and his abilities.

"After they meet you, I think they'll understand." Her sexy tone teased him. Tantalized him. But they had to talk first, before he lost all caution and reason.

"I'd prefer to elope, but I know you want to have your friends at the wedding. How about we plan a ceremony for here at the vineyard? The grounds are beautiful at night. We could dress it up a bit with candlelight and soft music."

"Sounds perfect. And when they see the setting, they'll understand why we're holding the ceremony at night. It's so much more romantic."

"I hoped you would think so. I'll start the preparations with my staff as soon as it's feasible."

"You have a staff? Do any of them know what you are?"

"No, my dear. We keep our secret as close as possible. My on-site employees in the production areas don't come to the house. It's fenced off for privacy and they know not to trespass on my eccentric wish to be left alone. I have a business office in the city. I go there sometimes—especially in the winter, when night falls earlier—for late meetings with the marketing staff. I also make appearances at charity dinners and such, keeping up the appearance of a wealthy businessman who works for fun and not necessarily every day. I have something of a playboy reputation which helps explain why I work from home and am seldom seen during the day. Once in a while, I'll brave the daylight and hold a meeting here in the media room. It's on the interior of the house and safe from the sun. I designed it so the interior core of the house is accessible without having to pass near rooms with windows. All exterior rooms open onto a hall that separates the interior sections and allows me to move about without difficulty during the day."

"Then you don't have to sleep all day?"

"Like anyone, I do need some sleep, and I'm lethargic during the day, but I can stay up if necessary. It's not the easiest thing, but I am ancient, my dear. Over time, I've gained abilities my younger brethren cannot claim. I can be awake during the day and caneven stand low levels of indirect sunlight for short periods, every once in a while. I don't dare go out of the house during the day, but I can always invite people here. Though I admit, I do look tired. My rare mortal guests probably attribute the circles under my eyes and the occasional giant yawn to my carousing lifestyle." He chuckled.

"You like having that bad boy reputation, don't you?"

He pretended innocence, enjoying her teasing. "It's a cross I must bear."

She turned in his embrace to face him. "Well no more, Atticus. You're a reformed rake now, and you'll be spending every night with me. Newlyweds are allowed a lot of leeway. I'll keep up the illusion around the house during the day—at least until I become...like you." She drew back to look up into his eyes. "Speaking of which, I want you to do it on our wedding night. I want it to be my wedding gift to you."

The very idea stole his breath. That she'd be so willing to give up the sun for him was humbling. Atticus kissed her, unable to put his thoughts into words and needing to express his undying love in the most elemental way.

He lowered her to the plush padding of

the overstuffed chaise, coming over her in a way that made her feel delicate and cherished. He had such a commanding presence, he overwhelmed her in many ways, but it was a delicious sensation and one she was surprised to discover she really enjoyed.

Atticus pulled back, smiling down at her. "So you like being my woman, eh?"

Lissa blushed as she realized their thoughts were twining as closely as their limbs. At times like these, the mental barrier Atticus held in place between them broke down. She felt his delight with the thoughts running through her head about his possessive actions. She also read the naughty images he sent her way—images of submission and tantalizing pleasure she'd only dreamed of to this point.

She considered herself a widely read woman and had even delved into a few erotic works of fiction. Some of the things that had intrigued her in those books surfaced in her mind as she saw the vivid images in her mate's mind. He'd done more than just read about those things, though he was cautious enough to withhold specific memories of other women from her. It was a wise decision on his part, considering their position.

Still, the thought of his vast experience rankled. Compared to him she was the next thing to a virgin.

"But I like virgins." Atticus leered at her in a comical way and she had to join him in laughter, punching his arm in a playful way. "Shall we play school girl and lecherous uncle? Or harem girl and sultan? Name your pleasure, sweet, and it shall be yours."

Unbidden, an image formed in her mind, even as her cheeks heated. His eyes flared with heat as he moved over her with predatory motions. She was his captive, and they both knew it.

"Ah, I see. You want to play captured lady and pirate rogue." He grinned and she could've sworn his eyes gleamed in the semi-darkness of the grotto. He looked around for a moment as if considering his options. "The setting is perfect, don't you think? I've taken you prisoner and we're hiding out in the lee of some Caribbean island. I like the way your mind works, my dear."

"Well it is rather...tropical in here."

"And you've read a good many pirate books, haven't you?" He winked at her. "I'll have to investigate some of those tomes.

Purely for research purposes, you understand."

She laughed. "I'd be delighted to assist with your...uh...research." He swooped in to nibble on her neck playfully, then retreated with an abruptness that left her gasping.

Atticus stood and offered her a hand up from the lounge chair. She followed where he led, more than willing to let him guide her in this secret fantasy.

He tugged her into his arms and looked down into her eyes, suddenly serious. "I'll spend the rest of my days fulfilling all of your fantasies, my love, as you've already fulfilled mine, just by existing and being here with me."

"You say the sweetest things, Atticus." She stood on tiptoe to place a gentle kiss on his lips.

When she pulled back, he bent and scooped her into his arms, carrying her toward the lush foliage surrounding the well-camouflaged pool. He made a beeline for a young palm tree that had numerous vines growing around it.

"You're my captive, milady," he said as he dumped her onto her feet and placed her back to the tree. He tugged one of the vines free and used it to tie her hands behind her back around the tree. "In short, you're mine. Best get used to it."

Leaning back, it wasn't uncomfortable. The tree supported her and the vines were strong, but soft against her skin. A few quick tugs told her it wouldn't be easy to get out of the bindings. The vines were stronger than they looked.

Atticus backed off slightly, surveying her. She was wearing a lightweight cotton dress that was like many she owned. This one had buttons down the front, all the way to the hem.

"A real pirate would tear that pretty dress off your luscious young body," Atticus mused. "But we haven't any spare female clothing aboard and I don't like my men lusting after what's mine. They'll do that enough just having you here. No need to make it worse by having you traipse around naked."

He was getting into this role and Lissa found it easy to believe he might've once been a pirate. As the thought flashed across her mind, she saw a tall ship in his thoughts.

"You *were* a pirate!"

CHAPTER NINE

"You'll soon discover that once a pirate, my dear..." he winked at her and tugged at the bodice of her dress, "...always a pirate."

He made short work of her dress, unbuttoning it completely and pushing it down her shoulders to tangle on her bound arms. She wore a bra and panties beneath. The bra had a front closure, so it followed the dress, sliding down her arms and getting stuck about halfway to bunch between her shoulders and the tree. The panties, he slid down her legs, kneeling before her as he lifted first one foot and then the other to remove them completely. With a devilish grin, he tucked the pink satin into his pocket, and remained on his knees before her.

Lissa shifted on her feet, uncertain. He had that pirate gleam in his eyes again.

"Atticus?"

"You're to call me captain, wench!"

Lissa jumped at the steel edge in his voice. He was staring at her crotch. When she noted the direction of his interest, he licked his lips, making her squirm. Reaching out, he slid one hand between her thighs, coaxing them apart. That hand rose up the inside of her thigh, tickling, teasing, tantalizing, until it reached the soft curls at their apex. He pet her then, watching her reactions as she trembled.

"Do you like this, wench?" Atticus slid one finger into her folds, stroking the nubbin that was already excited and awaiting his pleasure—and hers.

"Yes, captain."

"Say 'aye'," he corrected her in a throaty purr.

"Aye, captain."

"Good girl." He stroked her more firmly in reward, making her gasp. His fingers moved deeper into her secret folds, spreading, testing and pinching her with practiced finesse. "You're very wet, lass," he observed. "I think you've done this before, haven't you? I'll lay odds you're not virgin. Tell me, has your sniveling betrothed back in England been in here?" He rammed two fingers into her wet hole. "Has he had his cock in this wet pussy? *My* pussy?"

"No!" she keened, her head rolling from side to side against the trunk of the tree as he pulsed in and out of her tight core with his fingers.

"No?" He didn't let up, but redoubled his efforts. "Then who was it? The footman?" She continued to shake her head. "The stable lad?" He pushed her harder, driving her higher. "The deck hand on the ship I took you from?"

Lissa climaxed on his hand, unable to stop herself. She came in a rush, gasping for air as he watched in approval.

"Ah, so it was the deck hand after all. Tell me, milady, did you like it? Did he make you come like I just did? Or was it a fast screw against the wall?" He took his fingers from her core, but moved closer, using both hands to spread her lips wide. "Did he lick you like this?" Dipping his head, he made her gasp as his tongue licked over her clit, stirring her passions once again. He ruled her pleasure. It was as if her body knew only his touch and would respond to him in ways it had never responded for any other.

He delved deeper with his tongue. She

could feel his teeth beginning to elongate into the fangs that would pierce her skin and bring the brightest climax she'd ever known. He was gentle, but firm, and careful with those sharp fangs. He gave her just enough, never too much, but always just the right stimulation at the right time.

"Such are the benefits of sharing our thoughts," he said in her mind as he continued to drive her passions upward once again. *"And now it's time to fulfill the rest of this little fantasy."* He drew away just as she would have peaked, shaking his head and clicking his tongue in disapproval.

"You're a greedy wench, aren't you? With a greedy pussy that needs to learn who its new master is. Get on your knees, girl!"

Lissa was confused at first, but managed to sink onto her knees, her arms still drawn behind her around the tree, her dress pooled around her and under her knees, providing some padding. By necessity, her legs were spread, her ankles finding space on either side of the wide trunk.

When she looked up from securing her position, Atticus had undone his pants and was using one hand to stroke his hard cock, hovering just in front of her face. He smiled that devilish smile at her and she was lost.

"I can see you want this, wench. Tell me, did you suck your deck hand's cock? Did he give it to you day and night?"

"Aye, captain," she said boldly. It was time she started participating in this fantasy, she decided. Maybe there was a way to turn the tables on her lover. Eyeing him with a new, saucy attitude, she looked forward to trying.

"Naughty wench." He chuckled as he stepped forward, placing the tip of his cock against her lips. "You know what to do with this then. Swallow me down, girl, and do your best. If you please me, I'll go easy with the lash."

He'd surprised her with that last bit. Was he going to whip her? The thought should have sent her running for the hills, but coming from Atticus, the threat made her hot. There was something seriously wrong with her, but it felt too good to worry about it now as she opened her mouth and took him deep.

Atticus groaned when she used her tongue on him. She teased the crown of his impressive erection, licking and sucking until he was ready to come. She felt the tremble in his limbs, but he refused her. He pulled from her mouth with an audible popping sound as she sucked hard to the last second. She was disappointed, but it was forgotten when he reached behind her and released the vines holding her wrists and untangled the dress and bra to let them fall to the ground.

He lifted her to her feet and turned her around to face the tree trunk.

"Hold on, wench. I promised you the lash and the lash you'll get for being such a disobedient tart."

"What did I do, captain? I'll be a good girl. I promise." She was getting into the fantasy as he pressed her nude body against the rough bark of the palm.

"You gave your virginity to some slobbering deck hand. You gave away what was mine, wench." He used the vine to smack her bare back. It stung, but it didn't hurt too bad. Lissa was shocked to feel her arousal, which had faded a little while she pleasured him, return tenfold. "You need to learn your place and how to please me, wench." Another lash with the ropey vine landed on her backside, stinging the soft flesh and making her hotter.

"From this day forward you will fuck only

me. And those I give you to," he added as an afterthought before the next blow landed on her upper thighs.

"You'll give me to others, captain?" she couldn't help but ask.

"Impertinent wench. Do not think to question me. That's earned you another lash." And the blow landed in the middle of her back, lighter than the others, but just as exciting. "You won't question me again, wench. If I tell you to suck my first mate's cock while I fuck you from behind, you'll do it and no question. Do you understand?" Another blow landed while he awaited her answer.

She was gasping with excitement by the time she managed to answer. "Aye, captain."

"And you'll spread your legs for any man I choose to give you to while I watch, whether it be my first mate or my cabin boy. Do you hear me, wench?"

"Yes!" she shouted when he landed the next blow right over the crease of her ass.

"And you'll take me up the ass while the cabin boy licks your pussy if I ask it, won't you, lass?" He used the vine differently this time, bending it in half and riding it up the inside of her thighs, pressing hard against her pussy as she rubbed all over the tree, the vine, anything she could to give satisfaction to the flame burning her alive from the inside out.

"Aye, captain!" She cried out as he pulled the vine away and lifted her by the waist, positioning her on her hands and knees in front of the palm. In less than a minute he was pushing inside her, thrusting deep from behind.

"You're a feisty wench, love, but I'll tame you. You're mine, do you understand?"

"Yes!" She cried out as he pulsed within her, stroking deep and fast and hard, just the way she needed it. She was so close, it would take little to push her over the edge of the most intense arousal she'd ever known.

"Say it, wench! Say you're mine." He bit down on her neck from behind, taking her blood and stealing her sanity.

She screamed as she came, hurtling toward the stars in an explosion of passion unlike anything that had come before and took Atticus along with her. She felt the wet spurts of his climax as she twined her mind with his, experiencing his bliss as she shared her own.

"I'm yours."

They stayed that way, both panting and basking in the glow of a magnificent climax for a long time before Atticus stepped back. He lifted her in his arms and took her over to a chaise lounge off to one side. They lay there together for long minutes, basking in the afterglow of the most glorious love she'd ever made. The wide chaise lounge was soft under her bare body and Atticus was warm against her.

"Were you really a pirate?"

Atticus chuckled in reply. "Until recently, passage by sea was the only way to get from one continent to another. So, yes, I've sailed, but it wasn't a profession or way of life for me. Spending the daylight hours in the hold was often uncomfortable and hard to explain."

"I hadn't thought about that. Is it so hard? To live without the sun?"

"Sometimes it's the most difficult thing in the world. But sometimes...like now, since I found you, I wouldn't trade my existence for anything. You are my sunshine, Lissa. All else matters not."

"I love you, Atticus." She kissed his cheek and rested her head against his chest, closing her eyes, secure in his love. She drifted to sleep dreaming of the life they would have together.

CHAPTER TEN

"How's the job search going, Kel?" Jena asked over crisp noodles in a local Chinese restaurant. Lissa and her friends were having dinner together, as they had every few weeks since college. The old group had stuck together remarkably well over the years after graduation. Their married friend, Christy, had even managed to make their dinner this month, though she was subdued as usual. Carly, owner of a small but successful software company, sat next to her, picking at appetizers as the conversation focused on Kelly.

"Not good," Kelly responded, dunking a noodle in duck sauce. "It's the wrong time of year to get a teaching job. If only that other teacher hadn't decided at the last minute to come back from maternity leave. The school bent over backwards to accommodate her and hung me out to dry."

"That stinks," Carly said as she sipped her iced tea.

"You got a raw deal there," Jena agreed as the waiter brought their entrees.

"How's it going at the hospital? Did you get the cut in hours you wanted?" Lissa asked Jena after the waiter had gone.

"We made a compromise. I get more on-call time and less on-duty time, but the hours are still about the same. Killer. I think it'll be next year before I can really scale back the hospital obligations and pay more attention to my private patients."

"You know, even when you own your own company, it's hard to scale back." Carly sighed as she sat back in her chair and looked at her friends with weary eyes. "I'm thinking of taking a breather from the installations."

This was big news. Lissa knew all about Carly's work, designing and installing custom software packages. The job took her all over the country and she'd be away on an installation for weeks at a time. Lissa thought Carly had enjoyed the work and the travel, but she could see the lines of fatigue around her friend's eyes and the shadows beneath.

"You work too hard, Carly. I think it's a good thing to delegate some of the work to the people you hired. That's why you hired them after all." Jena wasn't shy with her opinions.

Carly nodded. "I think you're right, but it isn't that easy to get out of entanglements. I've got one more contract I have to work on myself out in Wyoming. I liked the area when I went to make the proposal. Maybe I'll stay there for a while and get away from it all."

"Sounds like a good idea," Lissa said, though this was the first time Carly had spoken about moving to another part of the country. Still, it didn't sound like she planned to stay there permanently. An extended vacation would be good for her.

They talked a bit more about their respective occupations, but Lissa kept mostly silent while the others griped. She had to break her news at just the right moment and was worried about how to phrase it, though she'd been rehearsing this scene for days in her mind.

"So what's new with you, Lis? Any more news on that hunky guy who saved your life?" Carly asked. She'd been filled in on the whole scenario, though she'd been away on a job when Lissa had been in the wreck.

"Actually," Lissa patted her lips with the napkin and realized her time had come, "I have quite a bit of news on that front. He asked me to move in with him."

Exclamations sounded from around the table. Some were disbelieving, some excited, but all were surprised. Lissa had been so caught up in Atticus these last days, she hadn't spared a whole lot of time talking to any of her friends except to reassure them that she was healing well when they called to check on her injuries.

"Well, are you?" Kelly wanted to know.

"This is kind of sudden, isn't it?" Jena, ever the most levelheaded of the group, seemed suspicious.

"Actually, I've been spending a lot of time with him since that first day I got home from the hospital. He's…um…I'm in love with him and he loves me too. We're going to get married and I want you all to be bridesmaids." The words came out in an excited rush.

Squeals of delight drew attention from around the restaurant as her friends jumped from their seats to clobber her with awkward hugs. Jena still seemed skeptical, but congratulated her along with the rest. They talked more about Lissa's news and the plans she and Atticus had made so far for the wedding.

Lissa was careful to explain that Atticus worked odd hours and would probably be available for a dinner one night soon to meet them all. In fact, she told them, he'd asked her to arrange a dinner party at the vineyard so her friends could see where she would be living.

Atticus and Lissa had discussed the plan at length. While the vineyard was kept private and as secure as possible, Atticus didn't think letting her friends visit under controlled conditions would be too much of a problem. They agreed to ease her friends into the idea of them as a couple, starting tonight. Atticus would pick her up at the restaurant, taking a few minutes to be formally introduced to the tight-knit group. It was one of many meetings they had planned for the next few weeks during which time the women could learn more about him.

When dinner was nearly over, an hour and a half later, Lissa gave Atticus a little wave. He was in perfect time to pick her up and meet her friends.

"Is that him?" Kelly asked, following the direction of Lissa's greeting. "Invite him over for dessert. We have to look him over and be sure he's good enough for you, Lis." Kelly's tinkling laughter followed her teasing statement.

Lissa rose, placing her napkin on the table. "I'll be right back."

She stopped on her way to ask the waiter to add another chair to their large table, then walked straight into Atticus's waiting arms. He kissed her with just the right amount of passion and discretion for such a public place, but refused to let her go completely as they walked to the table.

This was the perfect set-up as far as Lissa was concerned. Atticus could join them for an after-dinner drink. He wouldn't be required to eat anything, yet he'd be seen at a restaurant, which helped maintain his façade of mortality.

"You're getting good at this covert stuff, my love," he said in her mind as they neared the table.

"Every little bit helps, Atticus. I want to help keep you safe and if pretending to be mortal achieves that goal, I'm all for it."

He bent to kiss her temple with a soft brush of his lips. *"You're too good to me."*

He pulled out her chair and smiled at the group of women as Lissa made the introductions. Atticus was at his most charming and he easily won over Lissa's closest friends. Jena, the doctor, was the last to fall under his spell, but fall she did and by the time they'd drunk their after-dinner wine and nibbled on a few fortune cookies, they'd not only agreed to serve as bridesmaids, but Kelly had promised to help Lissa pack her belongings for the big move.

* * *

Lissa and Kelly had been packing all day at her apartment as it neared dusk. The plants were boxed, as were all the dishes and her mother's crystal. Everything but the kitchen table and the bigger pieces of furniture, which would be taken out by a moving company later in the week. Atticus had arranged it all. Or rather, his staff had seen to the details once Atticus had introduced her to them at a hastily called dinner meeting last week.

"Any news on the job front?" Lissa asked

Kelly as they finished wrapping the last of the knickknacks from her faux mantle.

Kelly sighed, sounding disappointed. "No luck yet. It's a bad time to be looking for a teaching job. I just hope I can pay my rent until the job market opens up a bit."

"Kel, you know if you need a loan, all you have to do is ask."

"Thank, Lis, but the situation isn't that dire yet. I'll let you know if it comes to that point, but for now I'm still okay."

Lissa would have said more, but the doorbell rang. She dropped the newspaper she'd been using to stuff boxes of breakables and went to answer it. She looked through the peephole, but the man waiting in the hall didn't look familiar. Still, the movers were supposed to send a guy out to measure things today and he hadn't shown up yet. Maybe this was him, running late.

Deciding that must be it, Lissa opened the door, but before she could even ask the man for identification, he pushed the door inward with a violent shove, sending her flying backwards. Lissa stumbled, just barely able to stay on her feet, though it was a close thing. Kelly came running as Lissa felt a splash of something douse her.

"I'm going to kill you this time, bitch!" The man shouted as he stalked forward, bearing down on her as she backed away in shocked confusion.

Everything became clear as time seemed to slow. Only the stumble had saved her from being hit in the eyes. She had no idea what the clear liquid was, but it didn't hurt. At least not yet.

"Atticus! Oh God!" Lissa screamed for him in her mind when Kelly jumped in front of her to face the madman.

"What is it?" Atticus was there, in her mind, quick as a flash, seeing through her eyes and sharing her thoughts.

"This guy's crazy, Atticus! He's threatening—"

"I see him, Lissa. Be careful. He could be a magic-user."

The man threw a chair aside as he stalked toward the women, as they retreated behind the small dining table in one corner of the apartment.

"What are you doing?" Lissa screamed, hoping someone would hear the commotion inside her apartment and call for help.

"You're dead, witch. Your kind are not allowed to live." Insanity looked at her from his wild gaze.

*"Stall him, Lissa! I'll be there as soon as I can.
And I'm bringing help. Remember, you'll have to
invite us inside, otherwise we won't be able to enter."*

"Just hurry!"

"We're almost there. Just a few more minutes."

"I don't know what you're talking about!
Get out of my house this instant!"

Lissa's strong words seemed to slow the
man. He stopped in his tracks and looked at
her with narrowed eyes.

"You can't fool me, witch."

"Why are you calling her that?" Kelly
asked. Lissa could see her friend was furious,
confused and scared out of her wits. It was a
combination she understood because she
was feeling much the same thing.

The man looked over at Kelly, pausing
for a moment. He traced some kind of
pattern in the air in front of Kelly's face,
then stepped away from her. "You're in the
wrong place, girl. With no power of your
own you can't rely on this one to protect
you. I'm warded against her kind of evil."

"Evil? What in the world are you talking
about?" Kelly drew the man's attention
again.

"You really don't know what she is?" The
man seemed suspicious as his wild-eyed gaze

slid from Kelly to Lissa and back again.

"No, I don't. Why don't you tell me?" Kelly was backing away and Lissa saw her friend fumble behind her back for the phone that sat on the credenza.

"Stay where you are, girl." The man's hand shot out and Kelly halted as if frozen in her tracks. Lissa felt a hum in the air that disturbed her. It felt cold and slimy, though she'd never experienced anything like it before in her life. It felt evil.

Kelly's eyes widened as she struggled to move but failed. Lissa was shocked. The man had done something that made Kelly literally freeze in her tracks. All with just a flick of his hand.

"Atticus." Her voice was a mere whisper of fright through their shared minds.

"I saw, love. He's the mage. Try to stay as far away from him as you can, but tread carefully. We're almost there. Just a few more seconds."

"Hurry."

The man turned back to her. "Now you die, witch." His features were grim, his expression maniacal. Lissa had never been so scared in her entire life.

"I'm not a witch." She had to stall. Atticus was almost there. She just needed to buy him a few seconds more.

"Then how did you escape my magic. You should have died in the crash, regardless of how hastily I set the spell. When I scented your power on the street, I acted quickly, but that spell never fails. You should have died."

"But fail it did." The man whirled toward the open door to the apartment and Lissa knew Atticus waited there with his friend Marc.

"Who are you?" The man sniffed and growled. "Bloodletter." The word was said like a curse as the man started to make furious motions with his hands. Lissa felt the oily hum grow again to almost deafening proportions.

"Invite us in!" Atticus shouted in her mind.

CHAPTER ELEVEN

"Come in, Atticus! Come in, Marc! Help us!" she cried, sobbing as the hum escalated, driving her to her knees.

In a furious blur of motion, Atticus leapt on the intruder. Lissa couldn't follow it all. Atticus and Marc both moved too fast for the human eye to follow, but in a matter of moments, the intruder was slumped on the floor, bloody and unconscious.

Atticus dropped him the moment it was safe and reached for her.

"Lissa, my love, are you all right?"

"Atticus." She sagged against him, burrowing into his strength as she shook in reaction. She'd never seen anything so violent as the fight nor felt anything as malevolent as that man's magic. It sickened her.

"He splashed her with something."

Kelly's voice came to her from beyond the comforting circle of Atticus's strong arms. "You'd better wash it off in case it's corrosive or worse."

Atticus drew back, examining her wet clothing. He smiled as he touched, smelled and even tasted the residual wetness on her skin. "It's Holy Water. Nothing more. Such a thing cannot hurt you. You're not evil and never could be." He hugged her close for a moment more, then stepped back, turning them both to face Kelly.

But Kelly's wide eyes were trained in dawning horror on the intruder and the man who bent over him on the floor. Marc's lips were bloody as he drew away from the attacker's wrist. There was no way he could hide what he'd been doing. Marc had fed on the man's blood and even now, licked his lips as he grinned at them.

"Magic blood is potent, indeed," Marc said conversationally as he dropped the unconscious man's arm back to the floor with a soft thud. "I have his essence. He'll never be able to escape."

"What are you?" Kelly seemed fascinated and not as distraught as Lissa would have expected. "What are you talking about?"

"I'm sorry, Kel." Lissa tried to catch her friend's attention, but she seemed mesmerized by the Master vampire.

"I regret you saw this, little one," Marc said, moving to stand in front of Kelly and touching her face with one long finger. "But there's no hope for it now. Much as I'd like to cloud your memories of this, I sense already that your mind is too strong to be swayed for long. If you weren't so close to Lissa, it might work, but you'll see her, and Atticus…and me, from time to time and the memories would resurface. You must swear to keep our secret or face the consequences."

"Atticus, is he threatening her?" Lissa asked him privately.

"Yes." The short answer came in her mind. *"It's the only way to preserve our people and prevent even more bloodshed. Kelly will have to be watched from now until the end of her days. She knows about us and that knowledge must be kept sacred."*

"Watched by who?"

"One of us. Most likely Ian. He's our enforcer."

"What if we watched her? I mean, she's looking for a job. You could give her one at the vineyard, couldn't you? Would Marc accept that?"

'It could work.' Atticus's tone was speculative as he placed a gentle kiss on her hair. *'I'll talk to him about it once this is settled. Ian's on his way. He'll take charge of the magic-user. We need to question him to find out what he knows. Right now, I want to get you out of here and back to the house where it's safe.'*

'I'm all for that. But we need to take care of Kelly too.'

"Marc, may I have a word?" Atticus left Lissa's side and took Marc off to a corner of the room while Lissa went to Kelly.

"What the heck was all that, Lis? Is your boyfriend a…vampire? Or am I losing my marbles?" A shaky smile hovered over Kelly's mouth.

"No, you're not losing your marbles, Kel. I know it's a shock, but Atticus is immortal. He saved my life after the wreck and we're joined. We can share our minds. He's my other half, Kel. My perfect soul mate."

"God, Lis. A freaking vampire?"

That startled a laugh out of Lissa. "I know, it sounds crazy, but it's not. I called to him in my mind and he came, didn't he? He saved our lives, I think, from Crazy Guy over there."

"This is all because of your psychic

ability, isn't it? Damn, girl. I always knew you were spooky with the things you could see sometimes, but this is just too much."

"It's part of it, I think, but Atticus tells me he's been searching for me for centuries. We're getting married and sooner or later, I've told him, I'm going to let him make me like him."

"You'd give up daylight for this guy?" Kelly looked duly impressed.

"Kel, I'd give up anything and everything for Atticus. He's my soul mate."

"Oh, Lis." Kelly reached out and pulled Lissa into a hug. Both of them were still shaking from the traumatic events of the evening, but it felt good to have Kelly's support. "I'm happy for you, though I admit it'll take a while to get used to."

The men returned as they let each other go.

"Forgive me, *ma petite*." Marc bowed slightly in Kelly's direction. "I'm Marc LaTour. I regret frightening you. That was not my intent." Marc's sparkling eyes hardened. "But it was important that one of us retain a connection to this man. By attacking Lissa, he has, by extension, attacked her mate, Atticus, as well. And where Atticus is involved, so must the Brotherhood be."

"The Brotherhood?" Kelly repeated.

"A loose organization of our kind in this region. I am the current leader. Atticus is my second. We protect each other and defend our privacy with zealous intent. Now that you know about us, you will be expected to hold our secret closer than any other you possess. Can we count on you? If not for us, then for love of your friend, Lissa?"

"I would never hurt Lis. She's like a sister to me. I promise not to tell anybody about what I've seen here tonight." Kelly laughed with a short, almost hysterical sound. "Besides, who in the world would ever believe me?"

Marc stepped closer, crowding Kelly's personal space. "There are those who would most certainly believe, *cherie*. Those that would hunt us and murder us simply for existing. That, I cannot allow. And so you must be watched for the rest of your days."

"Watched? By who?" Kelly's shoulders squared in agitation and Lissa feared the confrontation she suspected was brewing. She reached for Kelly's hand, drawing her attention.

"It's not as bad as it sounds. Atticus and I will be doing the *watching*. You need a job, right? Well, it just so happens, my fiancé here has a job waiting with your name on it. You can earn a living, work with friends and be *watched* all at the same time." Lissa looked from Marc to Atticus and back at her friend. "What do you say?"

"It is an elegant solution to all our difficulties," Marc put in.

"Okay," Kelly said, her gaze still suspicious.

"Great." Lissa hugged her to her side for a quick moment. "I'll like having you around the vineyard every day. Heck, maybe you could move in. We have tons of room."

Kelly held up one hand. "Let's take this a step at a time, Lis. For now, I'll take the job. You know how badly I need it. And thank you, Atticus." She looked toward him.

Any response he would have made was halted by the arrival of another tall, powerfully built man at the threshold of the apartment.

"It's Ian, love," Atticus said in her mind. *"You need to invite him in."*

Lissa waved at the man at her doorway. "Come on in, Ian. Thanks for coming over on such short notice." She felt strange to be exchanging small talk while an intruder lay on her rug, unconscious.

Ian nodded, making short work of lifting the dead weight of the crazy guy off her floor and onto his broad shoulders. Without a word, he turned and headed back out the door.

"Handy man to have around," Kelly commented with wry amusement. Lissa was glad to hear some of her usual humor creeping back into her conversation. The events of the past hour had been jarring, but it looked like they'd all be okay, including Kelly, thank goodness. She was taking all these revelations remarkably well.

"You have no idea," Marc agreed. "Now that we're all secure here, might I suggest we finish and head for the vineyard? We've had an eventful start to our evening and I think we could all use more peaceful and secure surroundings to talk things through."

Marc and Atticus helped them set the apartment back to rights and carried Lissa's bags out to her car. When Lissa looked around, trying to figure out how the men had gotten to her place, Atticus intercepted her thoughts.

"We flew," he said in a whisper in her mind.

"What?"

"Marc and I are very old. Over the centuries, we've developed many skills. One of the more useful is the ability to shapeshift. When needed, we can become whatever we need to be to get where we're going or accomplish our goals."

"That's amazing."

His wry chuckle sounded through her mind. *"Glad I could impress you, love."*

They headed back to the vineyard in two cars. Marc rode with Kelly in her compact while Atticus took the wheel of Lissa's sedan. An hour later, they pulled through the gate and onto the winding drive that set the main house far back from the road.

They gathered in the living room to talk through the events of the past hours. Lissa knew from Atticus's mind that this debrief was for Kelly's benefit as much as anyone's. The men would take her measure while they talked and they'd also help calm her and show her that they weren't monsters. Lissa was glad they were taking time with Kelly. Her friendship had always meant a lot to Lissa and she hated to think that Kelly's life would be adversely affected simply by being her friend.

Atticus was pouring wine for them all when the doorbell chimed. That was odd enough, given the fact that nobody could enter the estate except by being admitted to the gated driveway. Nobody *normal*, that is. If someone could fly, for example, all bets were off.

"Good reasoning, love," Atticus said in her mind as he went to answer the door. *"It's Ian. And yes, he can shapeshift into some amazing forms, including a rather fearsome dragon."*

"Now that, I have to see." Lissa resisted chuckling aloud, though she had to bite her lip to do it.

Atticus returned to the living room with Ian in tow.

"What happened?" Marc wanted to know.

Ian's lips thinned into a hard line. "The bastard put up one hell of a fight. He resisted questioning and when I gave him just a little leeway, he turned around and attacked me." Ian's clothes were scorched in places, Lissa noted. "He tried to send a magical message to his brethren. I can't be certain I stopped him in time."

"He's gone then?" Marc's expression

turned grim.

"No way to avoid it, unfortunately. I'm sorry, Marc. He was stronger than I expected and more than a little unhinged. He killed himself, in the end. His power turned in on himself and fried him to ash before my eyes."

"Damn." Marc twirled his wineglass idly in one hand.

"Did you learn anything before he died?" Atticus asked.

"Only that he was as mad as a hatter." Ian helped himself to a glass of wine at the sideboard. "And that he wasn't operating alone. He had at least one, possibly more cohorts. He also said he'd come upon your lady by chance. He was going to a conference at the hotel and noted her power as he waited to board the shuttle bus. Apparently psychic power is anathema to his particular sect of loons."

"That's a bit of a relief. It means he didn't know about you in advance. You were just a target of opportunity, not someone he'd been stalking." Atticus stroked Lissa's hair as he sat on the arm of her chair. "If he'd had more time to plan, you might not be sitting here tonight."

"I can't help but feel terrible that all those people died because one nutball had it in for me." Lissa felt the heavy weight of guilt settle on her shoulders.

"No, lass," Ian spoke from across the room. "Evil the likes of which you encountered tonight needs little excuse to kill. I have no doubt that madman had the blood of many innocents on his hands. The crash was in no way your fault. I've learned over the years, that some things are simply a matter of fate."

CHAPTER TWELVE

Kelly was given a guest room for the night when Lissa and Atticus finally retired sometime in the wee hours of the morning. Marc had stayed late, doing his best to charm Kelly, though she seemed somewhat immune to the handsome Master's charms. Ian left before Marc, but not by much, and he promised to return the next night to go over Atticus's security arrangements. Things would need to be updated now that Lissa was going to live in the big house as well.

Over the next weeks, Kelly went to work at the vineyard, performing organizational tasks for both Atticus and Lissa. Lissa moved in and Kelly was hired ostensibly as her assistant. Kelly took to her new role as liaison between Atticus's existing staff and the couple very well. Of those who worked for Atticus, only Kelly knew his darkest secret, and that one little fact, they discovered, made her invaluable to him in a short amount of time.

Kelly took over keeping the social calendar for both Lissa and Atticus. They attended a few evening events together and Atticus's business associates began to recognize her as his fiancée. Lissa kept odd hours. She'd sleep late after staying up all night with Atticus, but she did still go shopping and even sunbathing a time or two with Kelly and her friends. She wanted to enjoy her last weeks of sunlight before joining Atticus in his dark world.

It was easier, having Kelly to talk to about the changes she'd agreed to make in her life. They worked together in the house during the day. Kelly would work in the outer room of Atticus's home office, settling into the personal secretary's role, while Lissa moved her belongings over to the mansion and redecorated here and there. The women would meet for meals in the spacious kitchen or go out to enjoy the local bistros

All in all, it was one of the most enjoyable times of Lissa's life. She was planning the wedding with Kelly's help and enjoying time with her friends and the love of her life. It was tiring, to be sure, but she wouldn't have traded a moment of it.

By the time the wedding finally rolled around a few weeks later, Lissa would be a well-established part of the limited social scene Atticus enjoyed. The couple had established themselves as somewhat eccentric people who valued their privacy, but were still upstanding members—albeit on the fringe—of the local business community. They attended a few charity functions together where Atticus introduced her around and she furthered his façade of normalcy by appearing at a few daytime events, carefully chosen to enhance both of their reputations. It was a master plan, carefully crafted with Kelly's help and able assistance. Kelly, too, was established as not only a trusted member of Atticus's staff, but a close personal friend of Lissa's. When Lissa became immortal, they all agreed that Kelly would carry on her good works in the daylight hours.

It fell into place even better than anyone could have anticipated. But by the week before the big wedding, Marc had become a bit of a thorny issue. He'd started visiting the vineyard more often than he had in the past.

He'd arrive just after sunset to bedevil Kelly with barely veiled innuendos and flirtatious banter.

"Argh!" Kelly walked into the living room from the front hall, Marc following close behind, grinning like a fool. "Atticus, will you please tell your friend to leave me alone?"

Lissa stifled a laugh at Kelly's exasperated tone.

"Marc, leave Kelly alone." The smile on his face belied the serious tone of his words.

"What did he do?" Lissa wanted to know as Kelly flopped onto an overstuffed armchair that dwarfed her petite frame.

"He bought me a car. A Lamborghini no less. It's out in the driveway."

"What?" Lissa was shocked. She knew these men were rich, but she'd had no idea the Master vampire had enough money to give away expensive world-class sports cars to women he barely knew.

Marc grinned as he sauntered into the room. "Kelly and I were talking about cars the other night and she said she liked Italian sports cars. I thought she should have one, so I called Karl at the motor shop." He shrugged, seating himself on the arm of

Kelly's chair.

She jumped up and put space between them. "While I like a gift as much as the next girl, I can't accept a *car* for God's sake. I couldn't even park that thing in my neighborhood. You'll have to take it back."

Marc gave a long-suffering sigh as he slid sideways into the chair she'd vacated. "How about I keep it for you? I think I have one empty bay in my garage. You could come visit your car every few days and share a glass of wine and some cordial conversation with me while you're there."

"In your dreams, LaTour." Kelly's gaze could have killed a lesser man, but Marc was made of sterner stuff.

"But you are, *ma petite*. My dreams are the only place where you're civil to me."

Kelly threw up her hands, and fled the room in a huff.

"I don't think I've ever seen Kelly at such a loss for words before," Lissa said, smiling as her friend disappeared out of the room.

"No?" Marc asked with a speculative gleam in his eye as he watched the empty doorway through which Kelly had left. "That gives me more hope than it rightly should." He shook his head. "I have never met a more confusing, annoying and tantalizing woman."

Lissa nudged Atticus and he tightened his arm around her shoulders. He had to know from her worried thoughts how deeply the Master's words troubled her.

"See here, Marc," Atticus said. "I hope you're not thinking of messing with one of my betrothed's best friends."

"Messing with her?" Marc focused his attention on Atticus, his brows drawn and lips curved in an expression of puzzled amusement. "To be perfectly honest, I have no idea what I'm thinking of when it comes to the lovely and intriguing Kelly. She fascinates me and that is a rare enough occurrence that I'm driven to try to understand why. It could be that she is the first mortal woman in centuries to know what I am. That is a novel experience."

"Marc." Lissa sought his attention. "I think you should redirect your fascination." She took a deep breath for courage, but this needed to be said. "Kelly is one of my closest friends. I don't want anything bad to happen to her."

"I don't wish that either, *ma petite*." Marc's gaze measured her determination but she refused to back down.

"She's showing all the signs of being attracted to you, but I don't think it's a good idea for you to tease her. You could hurt her badly with very little effort on your part. Kelly seems tough on the outside, but trust me, she's got a gentle heart that bruises easily. I don't expect you to understand, but I'm asking you to leave her alone. She's had enough heartache for one lifetime already."

Marc's eyes narrowed as he studied her, remaining silent until she was about ready to fidget. Only Atticus's strong presence at her side kept her still and her gaze unwavering as it met Marc's. At length, he stood from the chair, nodding once in an old-world gesture of formality before he turned to leave.

"I'll keep your words in mind, *cherie*, but I can promise nothing except that I will try to comply with your wishes."

Atticus stood, gesturing for Lissa to stay where she was while he saw Marc out. Opening her mind a little, she saw through Atticus's gaze the sleek yellow car that sat in the darkened drive. It was a beauty, but much too extravagant for a simple school-teacher-turned-executive-assistant like Kelly.

Marc drove off in the fantasy machine

and Atticus returned to the living room. Lissa met him at the doorway and slipped under his arm to stand at his side. He hugged her close as she wrapped her arm around his waist.

"Do you think he'll leave her be?" Lissa worried a little as Atticus and she headed for the more private wing of the big house for a little alone time.

"I think he'll try, but I'm not certain he'll succeed. To be honest, I've never seen him like this before and I've known him for centuries. Never has a woman gotten under his skin the way your friend Kelly appears to."

Lissa didn't like the sound of that, but relegated it to think about later as Atticus guided her toward the more private parts of the house.

He led her to the master bedroom, which was in fact, only a façade. Inside, a hidden panel guarded the entrance to the underground complex and the protected chamber in which he slept. He would go there for the day, but for tonight, he planned to take advantage of the plush master suite and the giant bed he rarely used.

"Do you know how much I truly love

you?" he asked, each of them undressing as they stood before the extravagant bed.

"I can see it in your eyes and read it in your thoughts, Atticus. I'm more certain of that than of anything else in this world. And I know you can be just as certain of me. It's probably the most amazing thing about this relationship we have. No uncertainty. No ability to hide our true feelings. I love knowing that the man I love, loves me in return just as much."

"If not more," he agreed, sliding out of his own clothing while she removed the last of hers.

When they were both naked, they came together in a blistering kiss that rocked their combined world off its axis and in a totally new direction. There was no play this time, no teasing, just desperate need on both their parts.

Atticus had never known such pleasure. She nurtured something in his soul, shone her light on the seed of hope that had never taken root before he'd met her. Now it blossomed into a healthy, living, growing thing and his dark world was brighter for her influence.

He drew her down onto the plush bed,

settling her beneath him in the way he knew she liked. He could read in her thoughts how she liked feeling small beneath his body, how she liked his heat and his gentle touches. He gave her all she could take and more. He worshiped her with his mouth, his teeth elongating and scraping over her sensitive skin, making her shiver. He loved the way she responded to him. He'd spend eternity exploring new ways to make her moan and quiver beneath him.

The thought made him smile. He looked upward to find an answering grin on her beautiful face.

"This will only get better the longer we are together," he promised, licking her navel as her abdomen rippled in reaction to his touch.

"I can hardly believe it could be any better." Her words were a breathy sigh.

"Believe it, my love." He nipped her belly before rising to seat himself between her thighs. She was more than ready. As was he.

Atticus spread her legs wide, holding her knees propped up on his arms. He eased downward, holding her gaze as he took possession of her hot channel, joining them both in body and in mind. After the first few pulses, he wasn't quite sure where he left off and she began. He felt her pleasure and his own, the mingling of their minds combining and multiplying the rapture he felt whenever he was with her.

As they drew near the peak, he bent closer to her, folding her legs back to give him even greater access to her body. The angle changed when he bent even lower to sink his teeth into her neck, bringing them both to orgasm at the same moment as they shared minds, blood and ecstasy.

They lay together on the large bed, wallowing in the aftermath. Lissa stroked his powerful chest as she rested against him. She could still feel his mind joined with hers as it had been in those moments of shared pleasure—as it would be once she'd become like him and learned how to manage their mental link.

Her thoughts turned to her friends and how they would handle her marriage. Kelly was already getting into the groove of the vineyard and they'd talked about having her move into the big house so she didn't have such a long commute every day from the city. She would understand Lissa's new life better than any of the others.

Carly was going to Wyoming, so at least for the first few months, she would be out of the picture and wouldn't notice the changes in Lissa. Christy was habitually quiet and had to be dragged out of her house most of the time. Chances were she wouldn't notice any changes in Lissa because she wouldn't see much of anything.

Jena was another story. Sharp eyed and inquisitive by nature, Jena would notice things that others might not. Kelly would come in handy, standing with Lissa against any questions Jena might pose. But in the end, they were all her friends and they wouldn't hassle her if she was happy. And she *was* happy.

"And glad I am to hear it," Atticus said, giving her a lazy grin as she pulled back to look at his face. "Now still your racing thoughts, my love, and let me bask in this bliss for a few more minutes."

She wanted to be grumpy, but she felt the wonder in his mind of what they shared and she couldn't be mean. She settled her head on his shoulder again and closed her eyes, trying to relax her mind and release her thoughts.

A vision came to her out of the blue,

shocking her breathless.

Pain. Terrible pain and weakness. Danger and sorrow. Ripped, rended flesh and blood. Lots of blood. The smell of it was in her nostrils. The smell of death. Death and...wine?

Lissa shook out of the vision with an abrupt jolt as she sat up straight in the bed. Atticus rose beside her, his face clouded with concern.

"Oh no!"

"Was that a vision? Is that what you see with your psychic gift?" Atticus wanted to know.

Their minds were still joined, she realized, so he'd seen what she had. Looking up at him, she nodded, biting her lip to keep from crying. He gathered her close and rocked her in his strong arms.

"It's never been so strong before," she whispered. "Never like that. Atticus, did you see?" She trembled, remembering the face she'd seen through the haze of blood and pain. If only she knew what it all meant. The vision was nothing more than a warning of pain and blood to come, but it didn't give her anything solid to go on...except the smell of wine and the lone face in her vision.

"I saw her," Atticus confirmed in a grim

tone.

"How can we save her?"

Atticus held her tighter. "I don't know yet, my love, but we will do all in our power to help prevent *that*—," the anger and surety in his tone comforted her, "—from happening to your friend. I promise you.

# # #

ABOUT THE AUTHOR

Bianca D'Arc has run a laboratory, climbed the corporate ladder in the shark-infested streets of lower Manhattan, studied and taught martial arts, and earned the right to put a whole bunch of letters after her name, but she's always enjoyed writing more than any of her other pursuits. She grew up and still lives on Long Island, where she keeps busy with an extensive garden, several aquariums full of very demanding fish, and writing her favorite genres of paranormal, fantasy and sci-fi romance.

Bianca loves to hear from readers and can be reached through Twitter (@BiancaDArc), Facebook (BiancaDArcAuthor) or through the various links on her website.

WELCOME TO THE D'ARC SIDE…
WWW.BIANCADARC.COM

EXCERPT

Rare Vintage by Bianca D'Arc
Brotherhood of Blood #2

CHAPTER ONE

Kelly sat back in her office chair, staring at the computer screen. A heavy sigh ruffled the wisps of hair fringing her forehead. Things at the vineyard had been in upheaval since the Master vampire of the region, Marc LaTour, had moved in. Well, at least for her.

The blasted man seemed to be there every time she turned around, watching her with those dark, mysterious, ancient eyes. Since she worked in the evenings to be on call during most of the hours when her best friend, Lissa, and her new husband, Atticus, needed her, she had precious few moments of daylight when Marc couldn't corner her.

Just last night he'd dangled that damned yellow Lamborghini in front of her again, revving the engine as he brought it out of the mansion's twelve-bay garage.

"Just taking your car for a spin, *ma petite*," he'd called to her from the driver's seat. "Wouldn't you like to join me?"

"No, thank you." She'd been as firm as

possible and turned away as he laughed. The hardest part was she'd have loved to take a drive in the expensive machine. It was the man she needed to avoid if she wanted to keep her sanity.

She'd heard the sports car roar down the driveway a minute later. Marc infuriated her. He'd attempted to give her the car as a gift, which she'd flatly refused, but he persisted. He was like a dog with a bone, and she was the one whose nerves were being chewed on.

Kelly had moved in to one of the many guest rooms at the mansion a few weeks after Atticus and Lissa were married. Her lease on a small apartment in the city had come up for renewal, and she took the opportunity to move out. She'd never enjoyed the hour-long commute each way from the city to the vineyard. She'd been working for Lissa and Atticus since shortly before their wedding as the couple's assistant. It made sense for her to move into the mansion where she worked and one of her best friends lived. They certainly had plenty of room in the grand building.

Things had rolled along well until Marc showed up with the yellow sports car and a suitcase in tow. Marc had apparently decided, in his high-handed way, that he needed to move in with his friends while his own house was being renovated. Atticus and Marc were long-time associates and close friends.

They were also both immortal.

They'd known each other longer than Kelly had been alive. Centuries, in fact. It still boggled her mind to think that her best friend, Lissa, was now as immortal as her new husband. The thought of living forever was intriguing—even mildly tantalizing—but not practical for Kelly. Just the thought of drinking blood made her shiver. No, she preferred to live a normal life without the need to drink blood. Well, as normal as it could be when one of her best friends was a vampire.

Kelly returned to work, whiling away the hours until sunset when Lissa and Atticus would awaken. Marc, too, unfortunately. Not that he was unattractive. In fact, he was one of the most devastatingly handsome men she'd ever met, but he was way out of her league.

She sat back, staring at the screen again, lost in thought. Kelly jumped when a breath of warm air sizzled past her ear.

It was Marc, of course. He was hovering close, just over her shoulder. She could feel him, though he hadn't made a sound as he approached. Only now did she hear his slow breaths and the deliberate way he inhaled her scent as if he was smelling a rare perfume.

"I thought they made it clear to you that I'm not a snack."

"*Mmm*, I quite agree." He dipped his head lower, his stubbly cheek rubbing along her neck, raising goose bumps. "I imagine you'd be a full seven-course meal." He punctuated his words by licking the sensitive skin just over her rapidly beating jugular. "Ah, *l'aparatif c'est marvelieux*. A very satisfying feast for the senses at that."

The man had licked her! She could hardly believe it. She was barely suppressing shivers that wanted to course down her spine. It was devastating to realize they were shivers of excitement, not revulsion.

This had to stop. The man was a steamroller and if she wasn't careful, she'd end up flat. Flat on her back, that is, with him possessing every last inch of her body, her blood and her sanity.

"Mr. LaTour!" She twirled her rolling office chair around, making him move back.

"For the last time, I'm not on the menu."

His dark gaze blazed down at her, humor in its depths. "My proper title is Master, but you can call me Marc, *ma cherie*."

She rolled her eyes, putting on a brave front. "I call no man master."

To read more, get your copy of **Rare Vintage** by Bianca D'Arc.

OTHER BOOKS BY BIANCA D'ARC

Paranormal Romance

Brotherhood of Blood
One & Only
Rare Vintage
Phantom Desires
Sweeter Than Wine
Forever Valentine
Wolf Hills*
Wolf Quest

Tales of the Were
Lords of the Were
Inferno

Tales of the Were:
The Others
Rocky
Slade

Tales of the Were:
Redstone Clan
The Purrfect Stranger
Grif
Red
Magnus
Bobcat
Matt

Tales of the Were:
String of Fate
Cat's Cradle
King's Throne
Jacob's Ladder
Her Warriors

Tales of the Were:
Grizzly Cove
All About the Bear

Epic Fantasy Erotic Romance

Dragon Knights
Maiden Flight*
The Dragon Healer
Border Lair
Master at Arms
The Ice Dragon**
Prince of Spies***
Wings of Change
FireDrake
Dragon Storm
Keeper of the Flame
Hidden Dragons

Science Fiction Romance

StarLords
Hidden Talent
Talent For Trouble
Shy Talent

Jit'Suku Chronicles ~ Arcana
King of Swords
King of Cups
King of Clubs
King of Stars
End of the Line

Jit'Suku Chronicles ~ Sons of Amber
Angel in the Badlands

Futuristic Erotic Romance

Resonance Mates
Hara's Legacy**

WWW.BIANCADARC.COM

Printed in Great Britain
by Amazon.co.uk, Ltd.,
Marston Gate.